PAPERCUTZ ™
NEW YORK

GARFIELD & Co

#8 SECRET AGENT X

BASED ON THE ORIGINAL CHARACTERS CREATED BY
JIM DAVIS

GARFIELD & Co

GRAPHIC NOVELS AVAILABLE FROM PAPERCUTZ

GARFIELD
FISH TO FRY
& CO.
PAPERCUTZ

GRAPHIC NOVEL # 1
"FISH TO FRY"

GARFIELD
THE CURSE OF THE CAT PEOPLE
& CO.
PAPERCUTZ

GRAPHIC NOVEL # 2
"THE CURSE OF THE CAT PEOPLE"

GARFIELD
CATZILLA
& Co
PAPERCUTZ

GRAPHIC NOVEL # 3
"CATZILLA"

GARFIELD
CAROLING CAPERS
PAPERCUTZ

GRAPHIC NOVEL # 4
"CAROLING CAPERS"

GARFIELD
A GAME OF CAT AND MOUSE

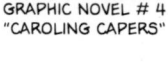

GRAPHIC NOVEL # 5
"A GAME OF CAT AND MOUSE"

GARFIELD
MOTHER GARFIELD

GRAPHIC NOVEL # 6
"MOTHER GARFIELD"

GARFIELD
HOME FOR THE HOLIDAYS
& Co
PAPERCUTZ

GRAPHIC NOVEL # 7
"HOME FOR THE HOLIDAYS"

GARFIELD
SECRET AGENT X
PAPERCUTZ

GRAPHIC NOVEL # 8
"SECRET AGENT X"

COMING SOON:

the GARFIELD show
UNFAIR WEATHER

GRAPHIC NOVEL # 1:
"UNFAIR WEATHER"

GARFIELD & CO GRAPHIC NOVELS ARE AVAILABLE IN HARDCOVER ONLY FOR $7.99 EACH. THE GARFIELD SHOW GRAPHIC NOVELS ARE $7.99 IN PAPERBACK, AND $11.99 IN HARDCOVER. AVAILABLE FROM BOOKSELLERS EVERYWHERE. YOU CAN ALSO ORDER ONLINE FROM WWW.PAPERCUTZ.COM. OR CALL 1-800-886-1223, MONDAY THROUGH FRIDAYS, 9 - 5 EST. MC, VISA, AND AMEX ACCEPTED. TO ORDER BY MAIL, PLEASE ADD $4.00 FOR POSTAGE AND HANDLING FOR FIRST BOOK ORDERED, $1.00 FOR EACH ADDITIONAL BOOK, AND MAKE CHECK PAYABLE TO NBM PUBLISHING. SEND TO: PAPERCUTZ, 160 BROADWAY, SUITE 700, EAST WING, NEW YORK, NY 10038.

WWW.PAPERCUTZ.COM

THE GARFIELD SHOW—A DARGAUD MEDIA PRODUCTION. IN ASSOCIATION WITH FRANCE3 WITH THE PARTICIPATION OF CENTRE NATIONAL DE LA CINÉMETOGRAPHIE AND THE SUPPORT OF REGION ILE-DE-FRANCE. A SERIES DEVELOPED BY PHILIPPE VIDAL, ROBERT REA AND STEVE BALISSAT. BASED UPON THE CHARACTERS CREATED BY JIM DAVIS. ORIGINAL STORIES: "SECRET AGENT X" AND "NOT SO SWEET SOUND OF MUSIC" WRITTEN BY MATHILDE MARANINCHI AND ANTONIN POIRÉE; "THE ART OF BEING UN-CUTE" WRITTEN BY JULIEN MAGNAT.

CEDRIC MICHIELS - COMICS ADAPTATION
JOE JOHNSON - TRANSLATIONS
JIM SALICRUP - DIALOGUE RESTORATION
JANICE CHIANG - LETTERING
GRACE ILORI -- PRODUCTION
MICHAEL PETRANEK - ASSOCIATE EDITOR
JIM SALICRUP
EDITOR-IN-CHIEF

ISBN: 978-1-59707-360-8

PRINTED IN CHINA
JANUARY 2013 BY O.G. PRINTING PRODUCTIONS, LTD.
UNITS 2 & 3, 5/F, LEMMI CENTRE
50 HOI YUEN ROAD
KWON TONG, KOWLOON

DISTRIBUTED BY MACMILLAN
FIRST PAPERCUTZ PRINTING

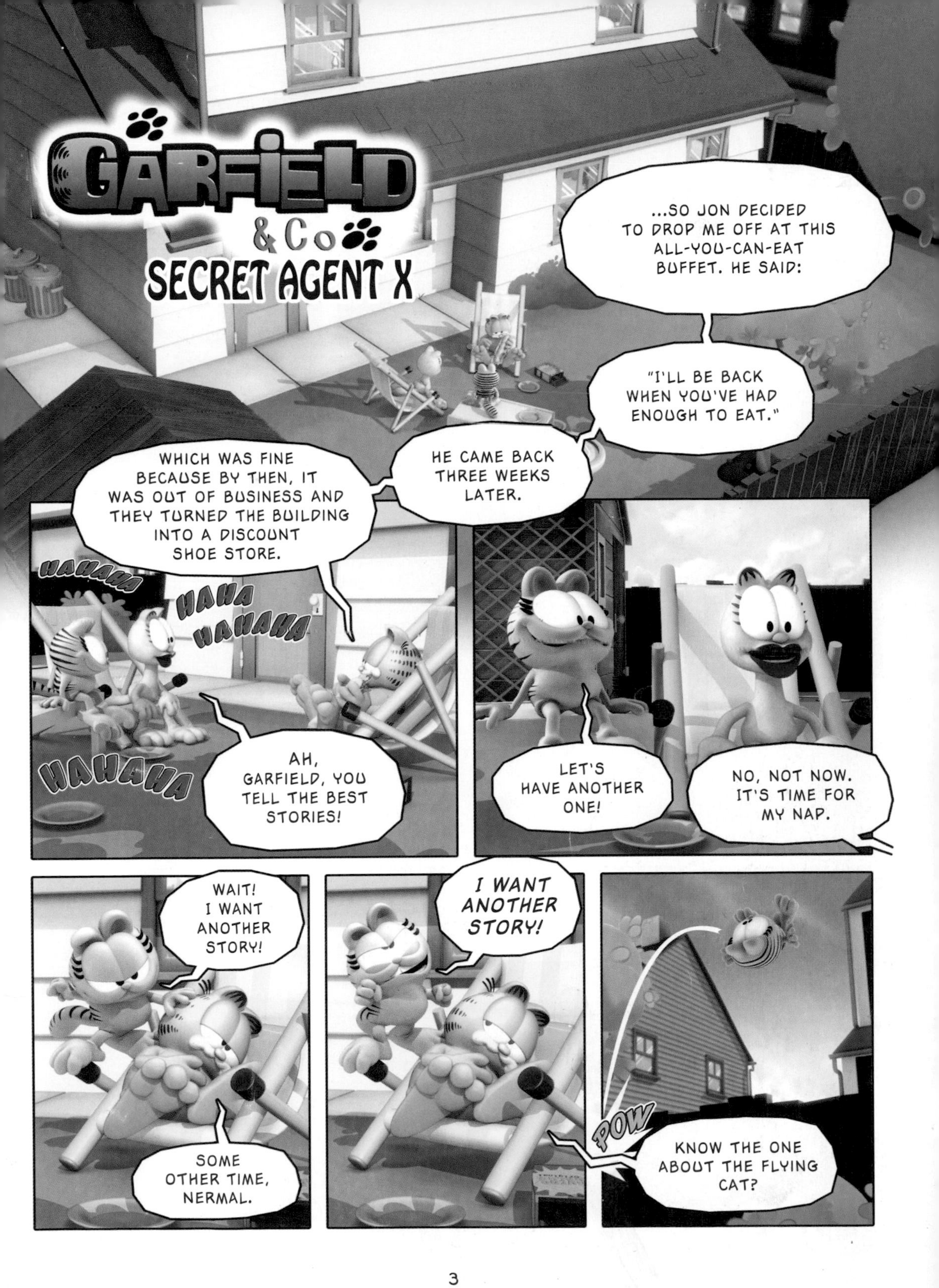
GARFIELD & Co
SECRET AGENT X
...SO JON DECIDED TO DROP ME OFF AT THIS ALL-YOU-CAN-EAT BUFFET. HE SAID:
"I'LL BE BACK WHEN YOU'VE HAD ENOUGH TO EAT."
HE CAME BACK THREE WEEKS LATER.
WHICH WAS FINE BECAUSE BY THEN, IT WAS OUT OF BUSINESS AND THEY TURNED THE BUILDING INTO A DISCOUNT SHOE STORE.
HAHAHA
HAHA
HAHAHA
HAHAHA
AH, GARFIELD, YOU TELL THE BEST STORIES!
LET'S HAVE ANOTHER ONE!
NO, NOT NOW. IT'S TIME FOR MY NAP.
WAIT! I WANT ANOTHER STORY!
SOME OTHER TIME, NERMAL.
I WANT ANOTHER STORY!
POW
KNOW THE ONE ABOUT THE FLYING CAT?

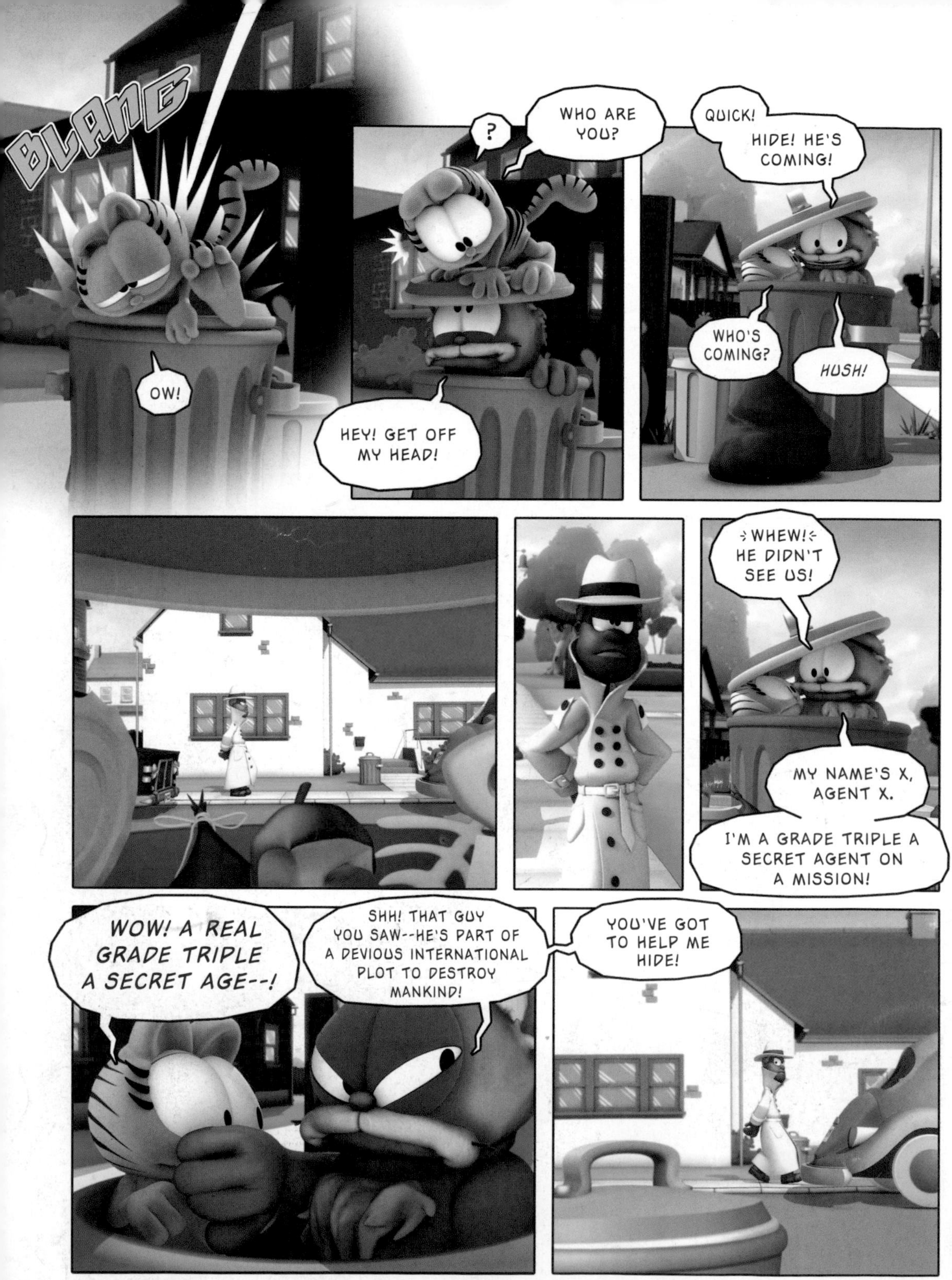
BLANG
OW!
?
WHO ARE YOU?
HEY! GET OFF MY HEAD!
QUICK!
HIDE! HE'S COMING!
WHO'S COMING?
HUSH!
WHEW! HE DIDN'T SEE US!
MY NAME'S X, AGENT X.
I'M A GRADE TRIPLE A SECRET AGENT ON A MISSION!
WOW! A REAL GRADE TRIPLE A SECRET AGE--!
SHH! THAT GUY YOU SAW--HE'S PART OF A DEVIOUS INTERNATIONAL PLOT TO DESTROY MANKIND!
YOU'VE GOT TO HELP ME HIDE!

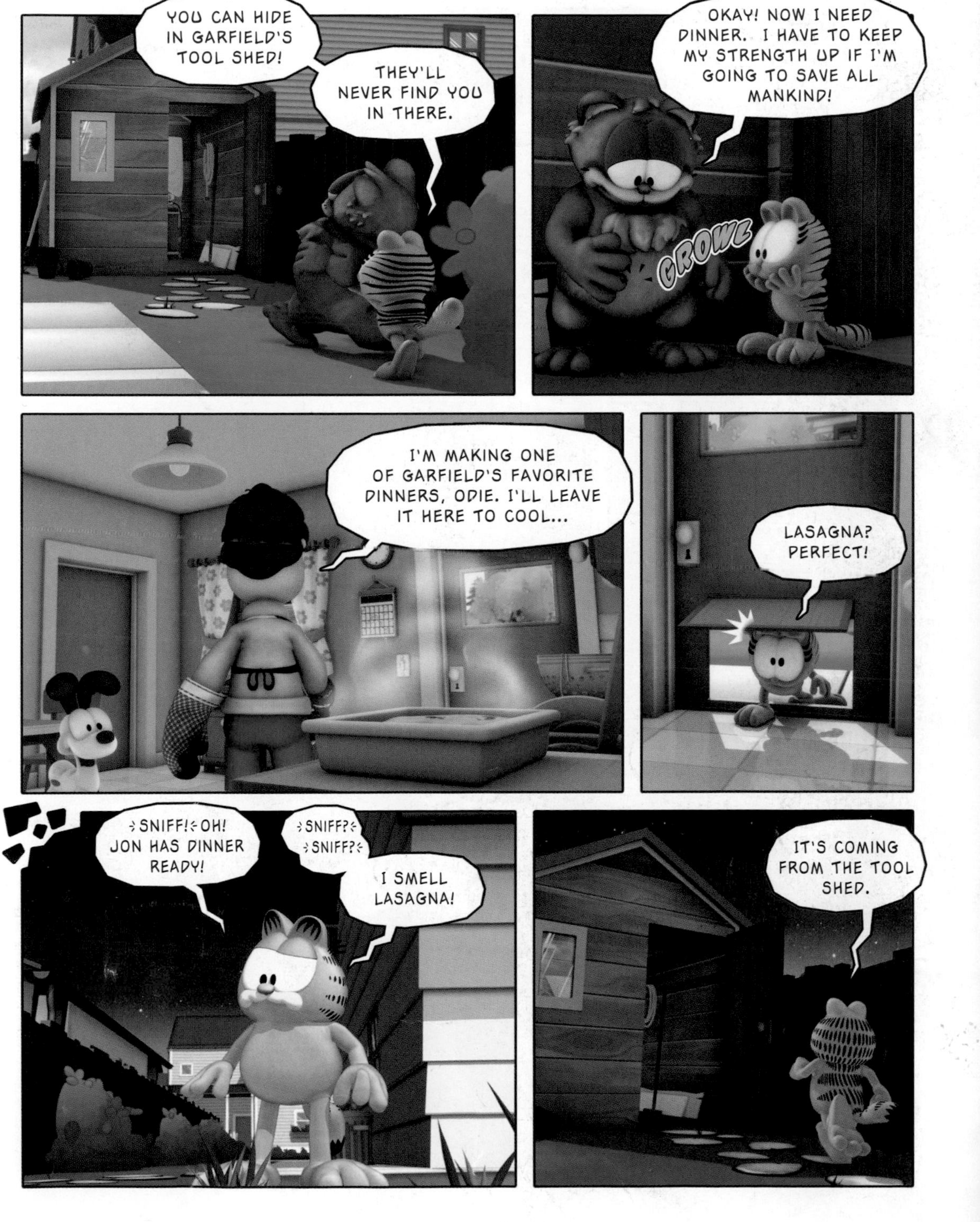
YOU CAN HIDE IN GARFIELD'S TOOL SHED!
THEY'LL NEVER FIND YOU IN THERE.
OKAY! NOW I NEED DINNER. I HAVE TO KEEP MY STRENGTH UP IF I'M GOING TO SAVE ALL MANKIND!
GROWL
I'M MAKING ONE OF GARFIELD'S FAVORITE DINNERS, ODIE. I'LL LEAVE IT HERE TO COOL...
LASAGNA? PERFECT!
SNIFF! OH! JON HAS DINNER READY!
SNIFF? SNIFF?
I SMELL LASAGNA!
IT'S COMING FROM THE TOOL SHED.

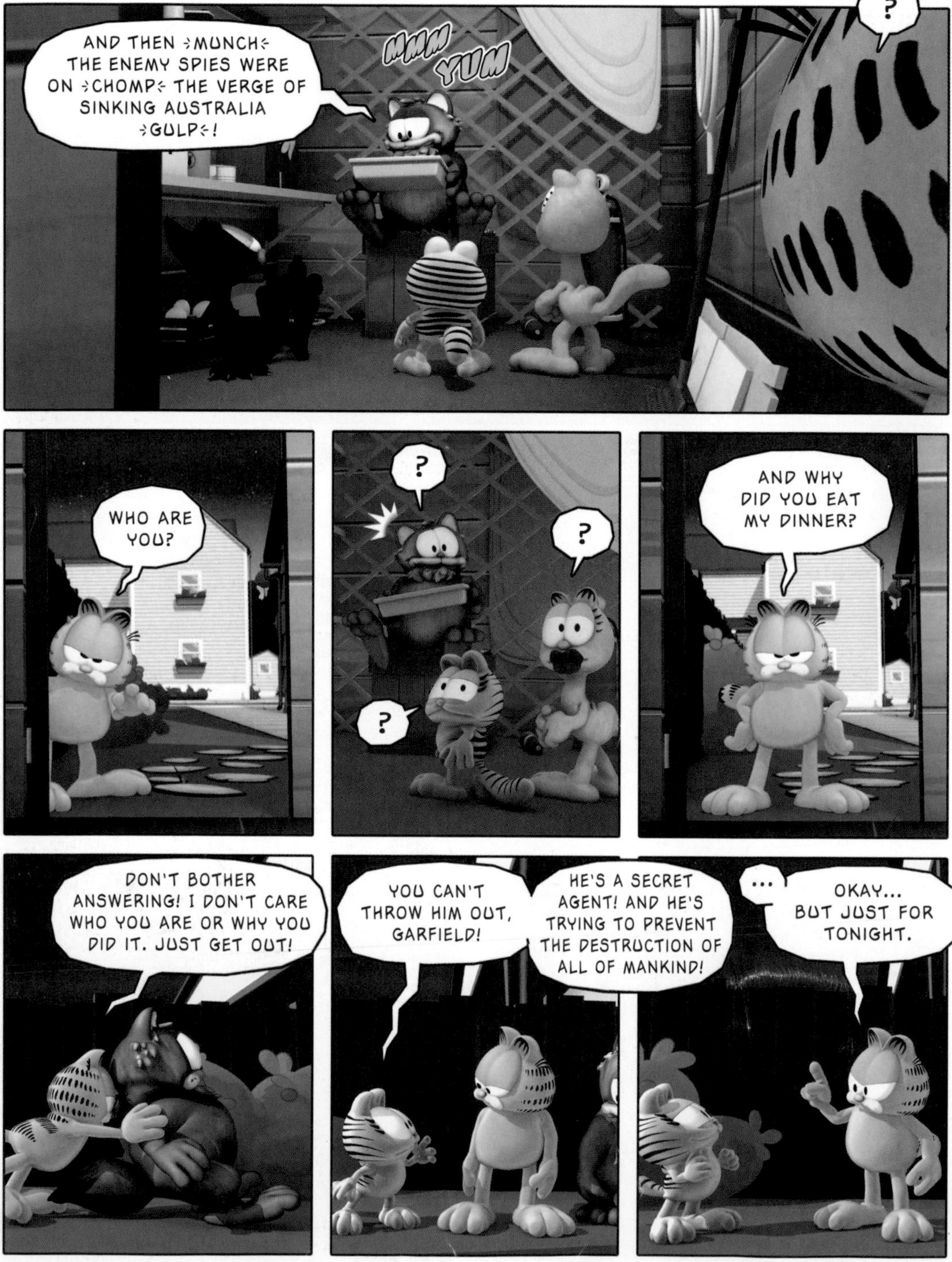
AND THEN ⇛MUNCH⇚ THE ENEMY SPIES WERE ON ⇛CHOMP⇚ THE VERGE OF SINKING AUSTRALIA ⇛GULP⇚!
MMM YUM
?
WHO ARE YOU?
?
?
?
AND WHY DID YOU EAT MY DINNER?
DON'T BOTHER ANSWERING! I DON'T CARE WHO YOU ARE OR WHY YOU DID IT. JUST GET OUT!
YOU CAN'T THROW HIM OUT, GARFIELD!
HE'S A SECRET AGENT! AND HE'S TRYING TO PREVENT THE DESTRUCTION OF ALL OF MANKIND!
...
OKAY... BUT JUST FOR TONIGHT.

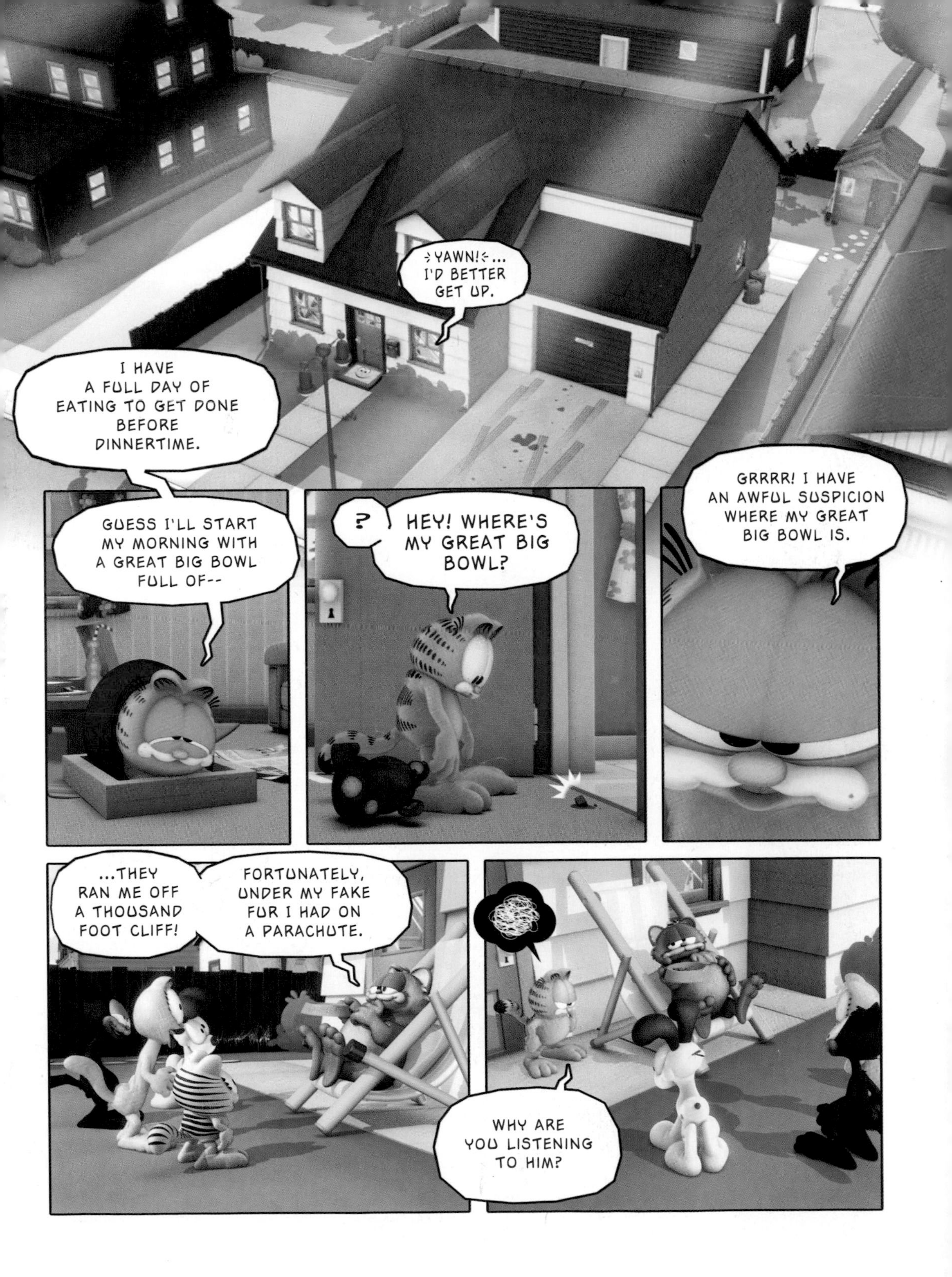
⊰YAWN!⊱... I'D BETTER GET UP.
I HAVE A FULL DAY OF EATING TO GET DONE BEFORE DINNERTIME.
GUESS I'LL START MY MORNING WITH A GREAT BIG BOWL FULL OF--
?
HEY! WHERE'S MY GREAT BIG BOWL?
GRRRR! I HAVE AN AWFUL SUSPICION WHERE MY GREAT BIG BOWL IS.
...THEY RAN ME OFF A THOUSAND FOOT CLIFF!
FORTUNATELY, UNDER MY FAKE FUR I HAD ON A PARACHUTE.
WHY ARE YOU LISTENING TO HIM?

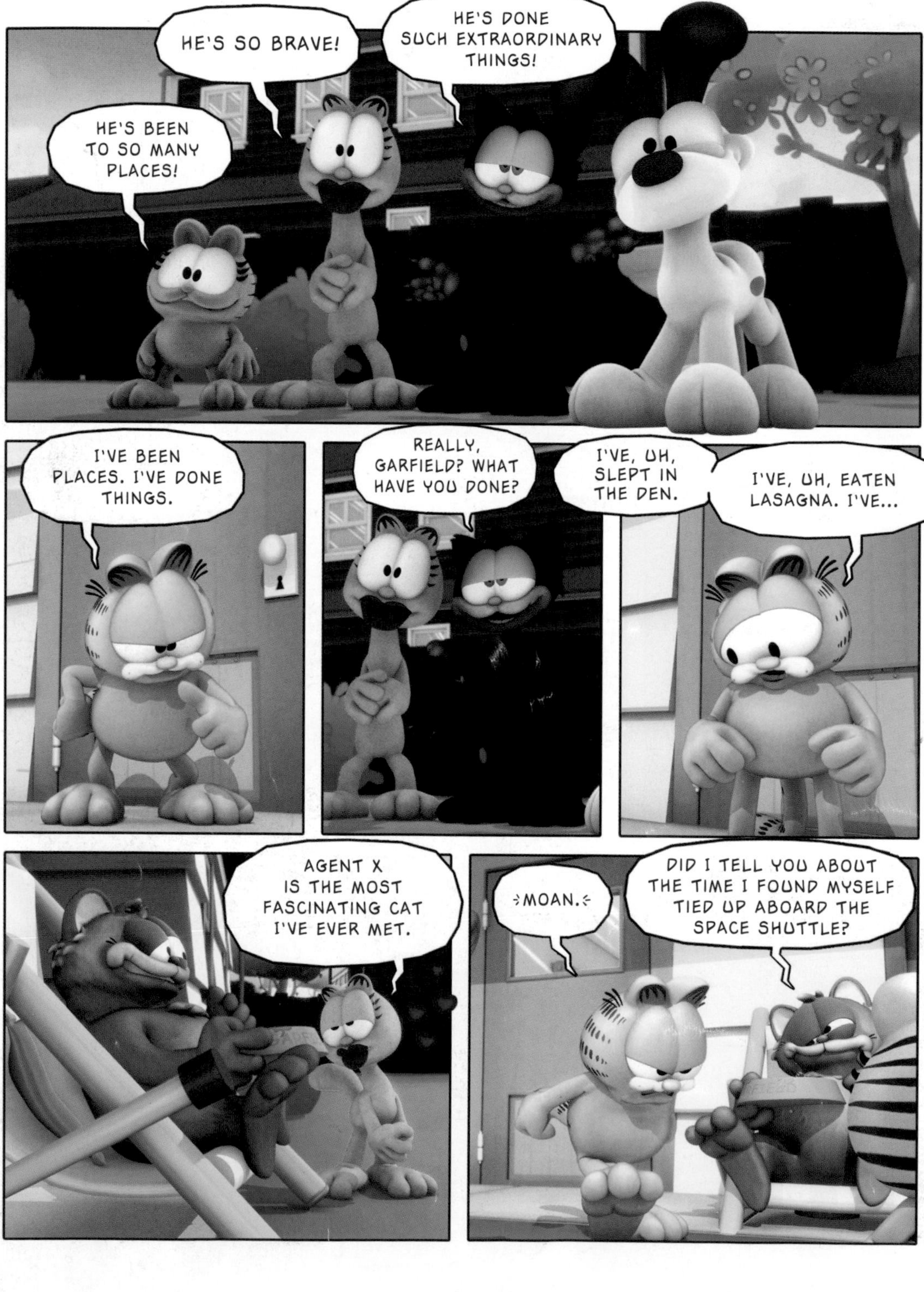
HE'S BEEN TO SO MANY PLACES!
HE'S SO BRAVE!
HE'S DONE SUCH EXTRAORDINARY THINGS!
I'VE BEEN PLACES. I'VE DONE THINGS.
REALLY, GARFIELD? WHAT HAVE YOU DONE?
I'VE, UH, SLEPT IN THE DEN.
I'VE, UH, EATEN LASAGNA. I'VE...
AGENT X IS THE MOST FASCINATING CAT I'VE EVER MET.
DID I TELL YOU ABOUT THE TIME I FOUND MYSELF TIED UP ABOARD THE SPACE SHUTTLE?
MOAN.

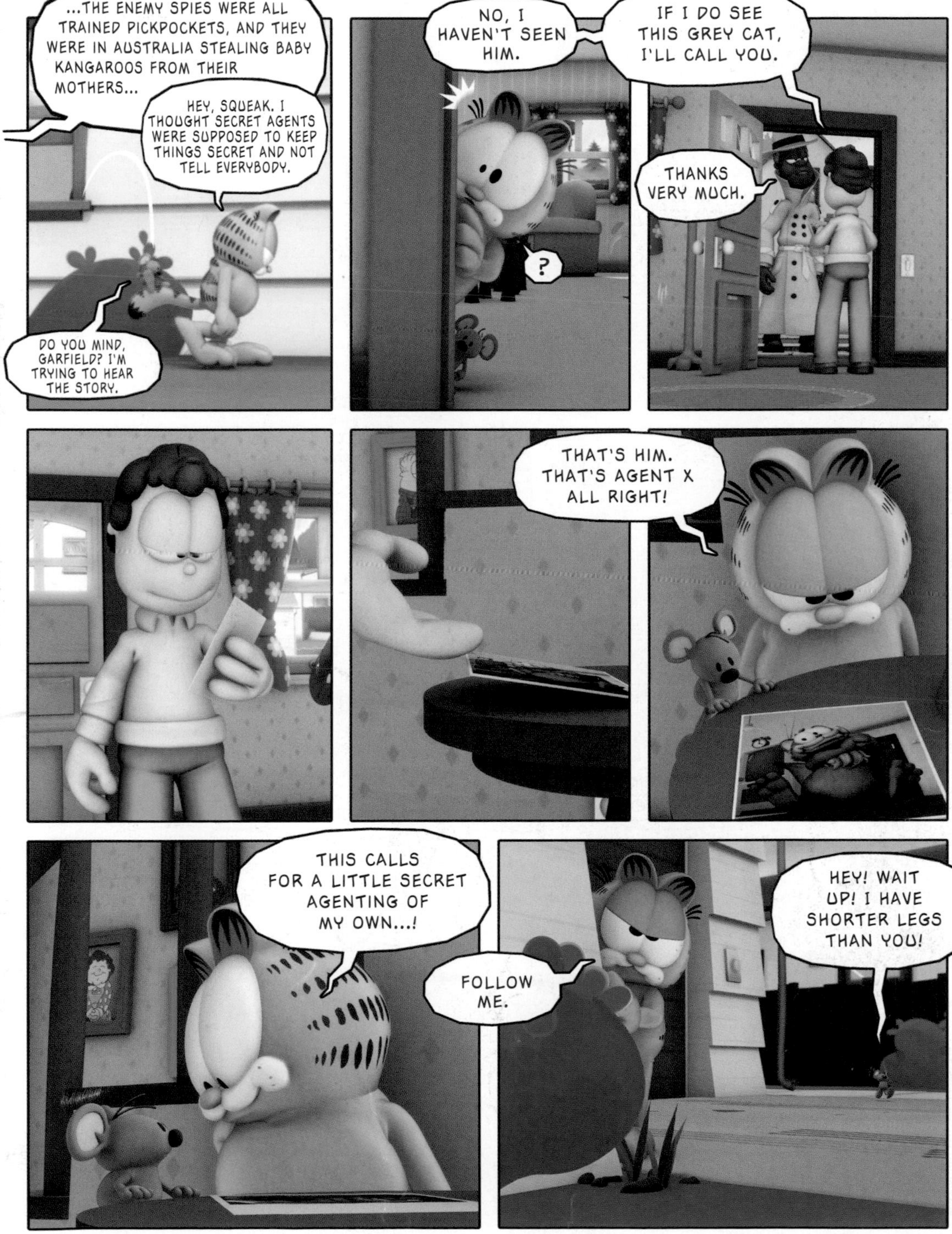
...THE ENEMY SPIES WERE ALL TRAINED PICKPOCKETS, AND THEY WERE IN AUSTRALIA STEALING BABY KANGAROOS FROM THEIR MOTHERS...
HEY, SQUEAK. I THOUGHT SECRET AGENTS WERE SUPPOSED TO KEEP THINGS SECRET AND NOT TELL EVERYBODY.
DO YOU MIND, GARFIELD? I'M TRYING TO HEAR THE STORY.
NO, I HAVEN'T SEEN HIM.
IF I DO SEE THIS GREY CAT, I'LL CALL YOU.
?
THANKS VERY MUCH.
THAT'S HIM. THAT'S AGENT X ALL RIGHT!
THIS CALLS FOR A LITTLE SECRET AGENTING OF MY OWN...!
FOLLOW ME.
HEY! WAIT UP! I HAVE SHORTER LEGS THAN YOU!

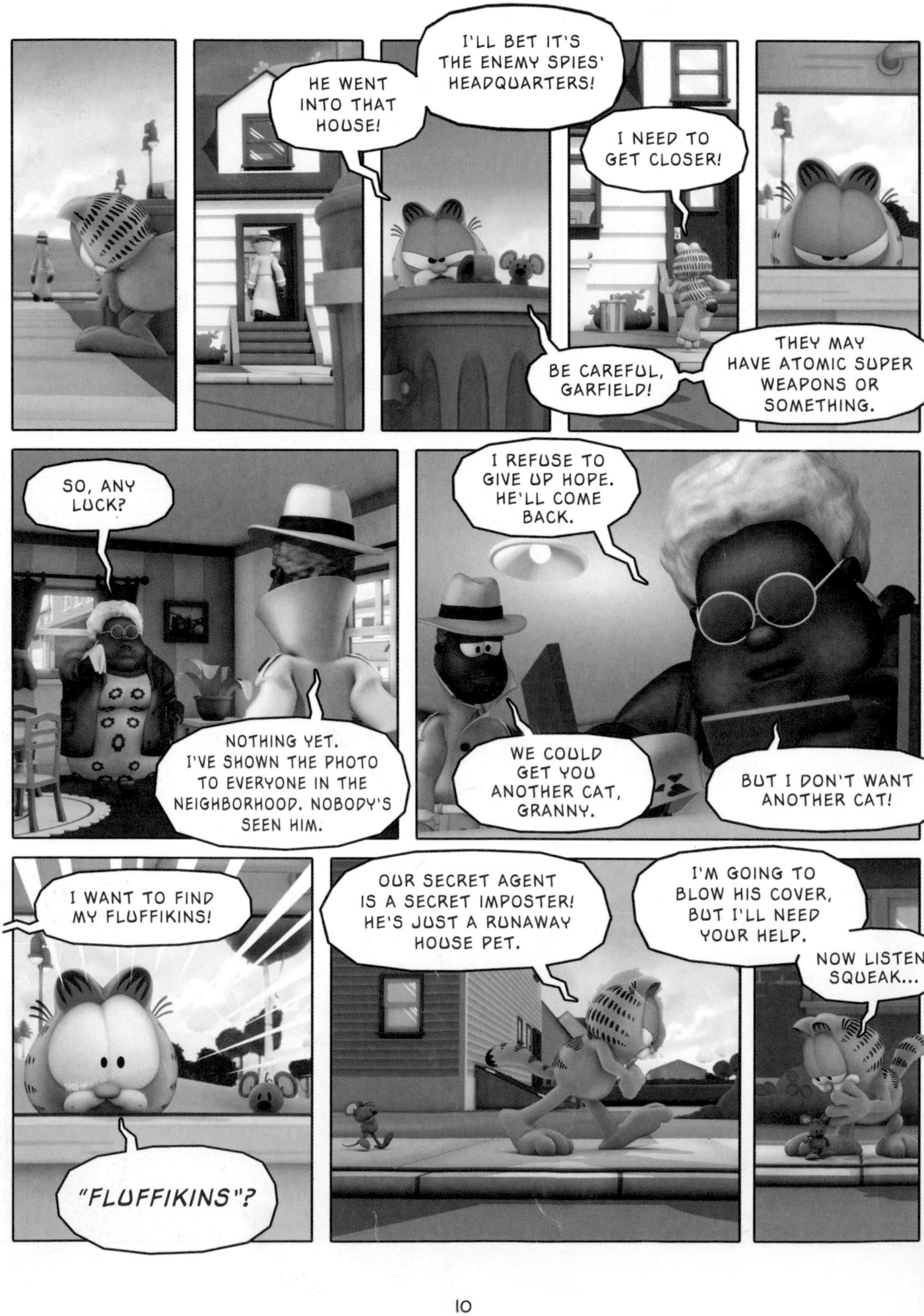
HE WENT INTO THAT HOUSE!
I'LL BET IT'S THE ENEMY SPIES' HEADQUARTERS!
I NEED TO GET CLOSER!
BE CAREFUL, GARFIELD!
THEY MAY HAVE ATOMIC SUPER WEAPONS OR SOMETHING.
SO, ANY LUCK?
NOTHING YET. I'VE SHOWN THE PHOTO TO EVERYONE IN THE NEIGHBORHOOD. NOBODY'S SEEN HIM.
I REFUSE TO GIVE UP HOPE. HE'LL COME BACK.
WE COULD GET YOU ANOTHER CAT, GRANNY.
BUT I DON'T WANT ANOTHER CAT!
I WANT TO FIND MY FLUFFIKINS!
"FLUFFIKINS"?
OUR SECRET AGENT IS A SECRET IMPOSTER! HE'S JUST A RUNAWAY HOUSE PET.
I'M GOING TO BLOW HIS COVER, BUT I'LL NEED YOUR HELP.
NOW LISTEN, SQUEAK...

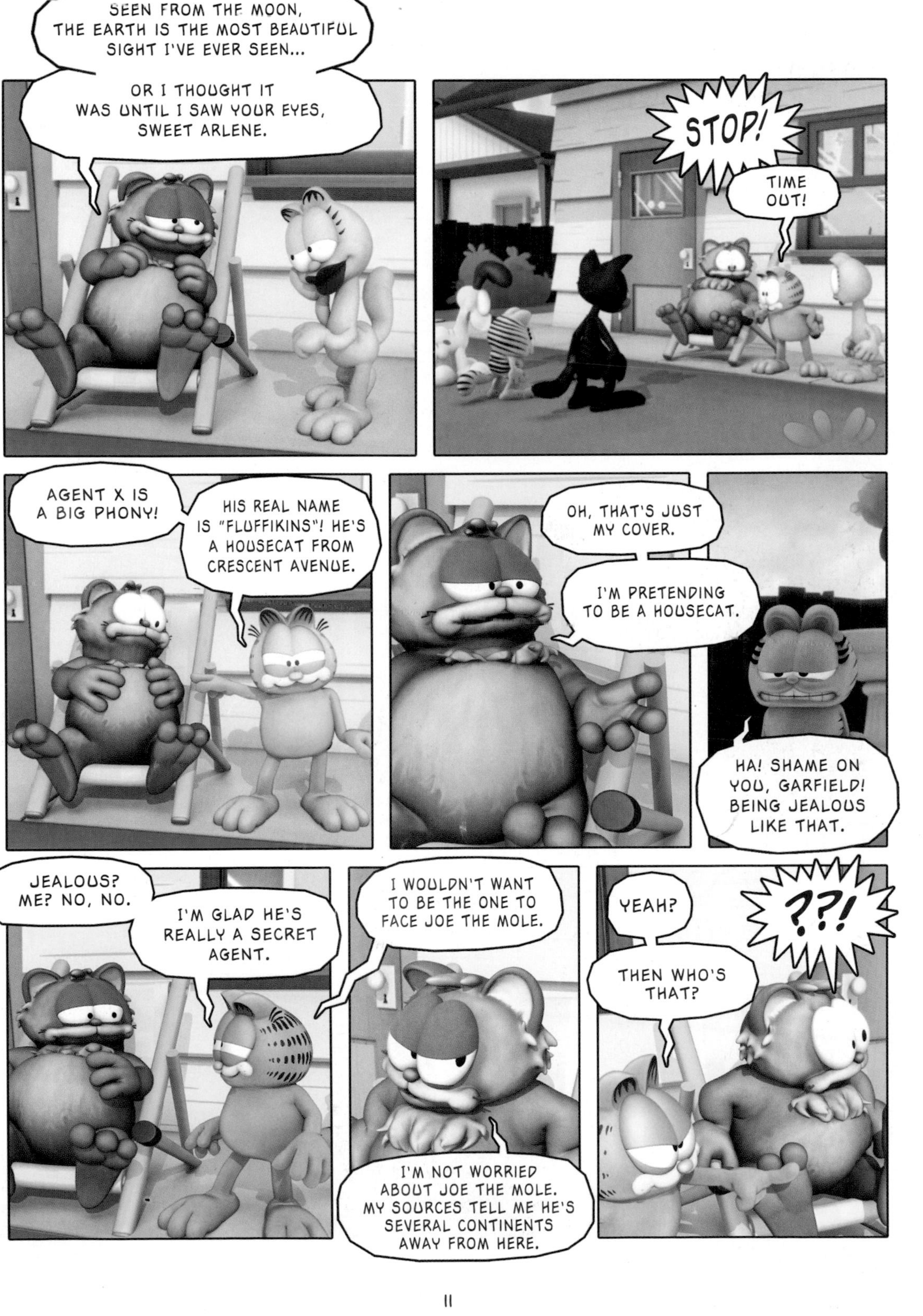
SEEN FROM THE MOON, THE EARTH IS THE MOST BEAUTIFUL SIGHT I'VE EVER SEEN...
OR I THOUGHT IT WAS UNTIL I SAW YOUR EYES, SWEET ARLENE.
STOP!
TIME OUT!
AGENT X IS A BIG PHONY!
HIS REAL NAME IS "FLUFFIKINS"! HE'S A HOUSECAT FROM CRESCENT AVENUE.
OH, THAT'S JUST MY COVER.
I'M PRETENDING TO BE A HOUSECAT.
HA! SHAME ON YOU, GARFIELD! BEING JEALOUS LIKE THAT.
JEALOUS? ME? NO, NO.
I'M GLAD HE'S REALLY A SECRET AGENT.
I WOULDN'T WANT TO BE THE ONE TO FACE JOE THE MOLE.
I'M NOT WORRIED ABOUT JOE THE MOLE. MY SOURCES TELL ME HE'S SEVERAL CONTINENTS AWAY FROM HERE.
YEAH?
THEN WHO'S THAT?
??!

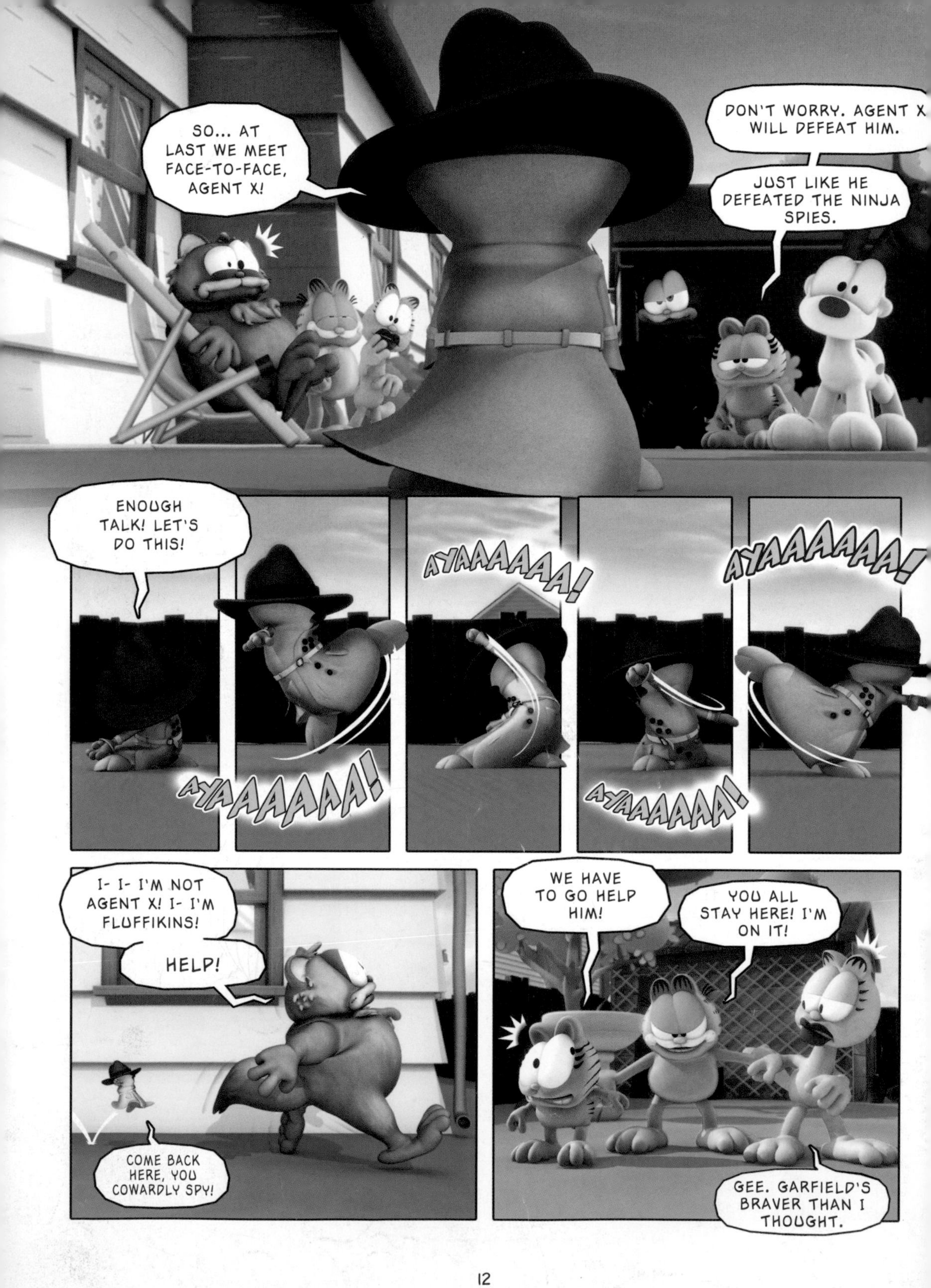

SO... AT LAST WE MEET FACE-TO-FACE, AGENT X!
DON'T WORRY. AGENT X WILL DEFEAT HIM.
JUST LIKE HE DEFEATED THE NINJA SPIES.
ENOUGH TALK! LET'S DO THIS!
AYAAAAAAA!
AYAAAAAAA!
AYAAAAAAA!
AYAAAAAAA!
I- I- I'M NOT AGENT X! I- I'M FLUFFIKINS!
HELP!
COME BACK HERE, YOU COWARDLY SPY!
WE HAVE TO GO HELP HIM!
YOU ALL STAY HERE! I'M ON IT!
GEE. GARFIELD'S BRAVER THAN I THOUGHT.

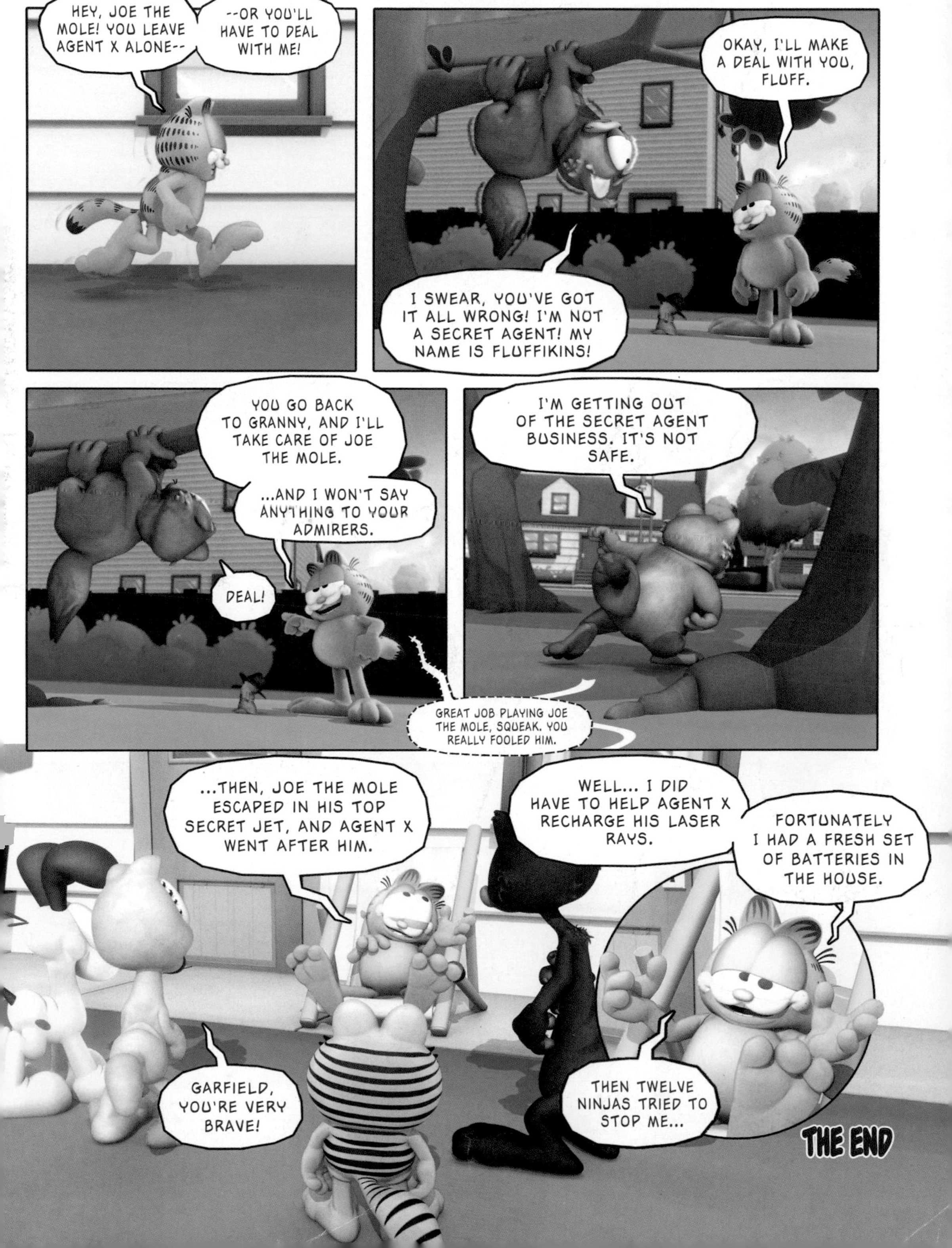
HEY, JOE THE MOLE! YOU LEAVE AGENT X ALONE--
--OR YOU'LL HAVE TO DEAL WITH ME!
OKAY, I'LL MAKE A DEAL WITH YOU, FLUFF.
I SWEAR, YOU'VE GOT IT ALL WRONG! I'M NOT A SECRET AGENT! MY NAME IS FLUFFIKINS!
YOU GO BACK TO GRANNY, AND I'LL TAKE CARE OF JOE THE MOLE.
...AND I WON'T SAY ANYTHING TO YOUR ADMIRERS.
DEAL!
I'M GETTING OUT OF THE SECRET AGENT BUSINESS. IT'S NOT SAFE.
GREAT JOB PLAYING JOE THE MOLE, SQUEAK. YOU REALLY FOOLED HIM.
...THEN, JOE THE MOLE ESCAPED IN HIS TOP SECRET JET, AND AGENT X WENT AFTER HIM.
WELL... I DID HAVE TO HELP AGENT X RECHARGE HIS LASER RAYS.
FORTUNATELY I HAD A FRESH SET OF BATTERIES IN THE HOUSE.
GARFIELD, YOU'RE VERY BRAVE!
THEN TWELVE NINJAS TRIED TO STOP ME...
THE END

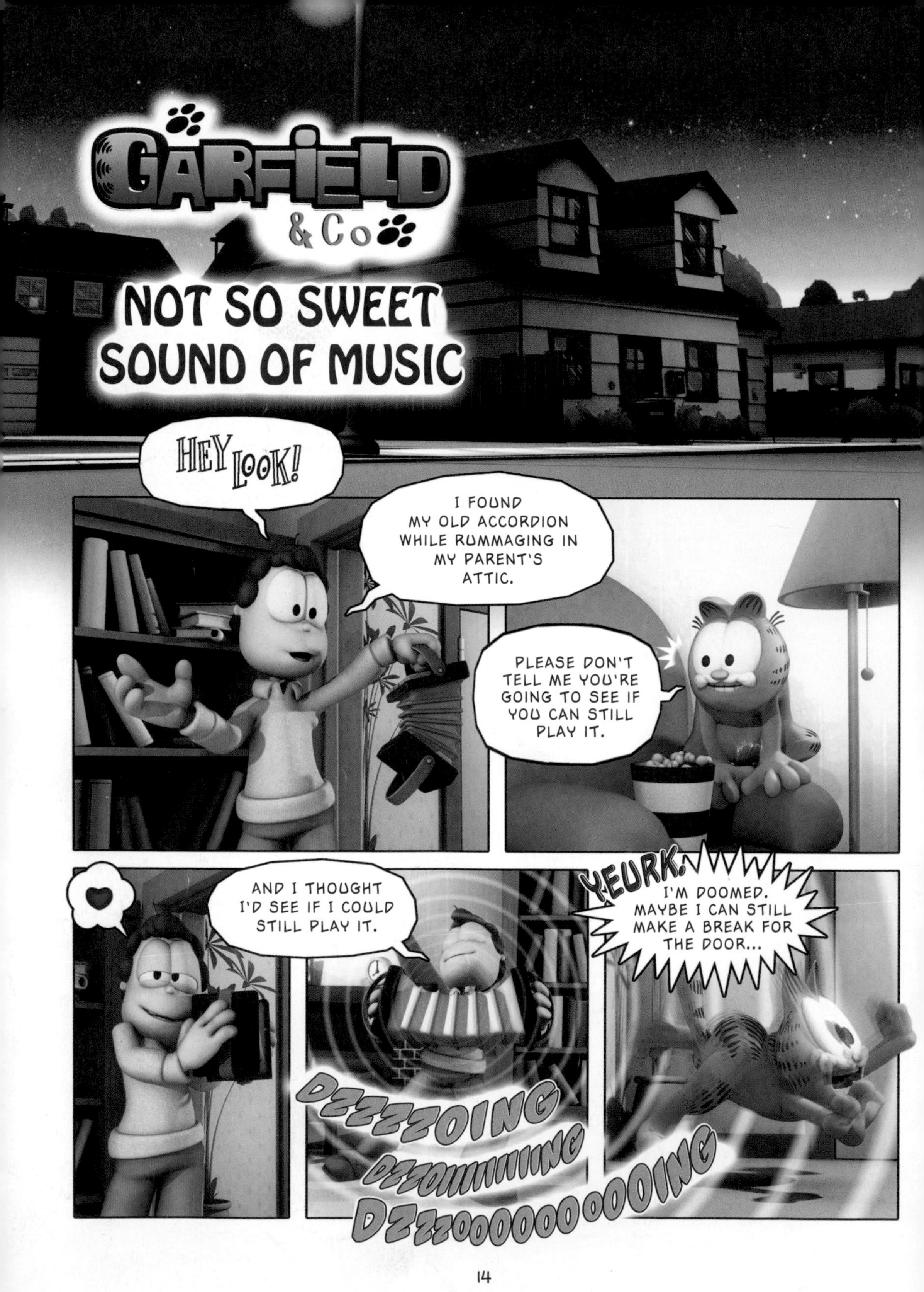
GARFIELD & Co
NOT SO SWEET SOUND OF MUSIC
HEY LOOK!
I FOUND MY OLD ACCORDION WHILE RUMMAGING IN MY PARENT'S ATTIC.
PLEASE DON'T TELL ME YOU'RE GOING TO SEE IF YOU CAN STILL PLAY IT.
AND I THOUGHT I'D SEE IF I COULD STILL PLAY IT.
YEURK.
I'M DOOMED. MAYBE I CAN STILL MAKE A BREAK FOR THE DOOR...
DZZZZZOING
DZZOIIIIIIIIIING
DZZZOOOOOOOOOOING

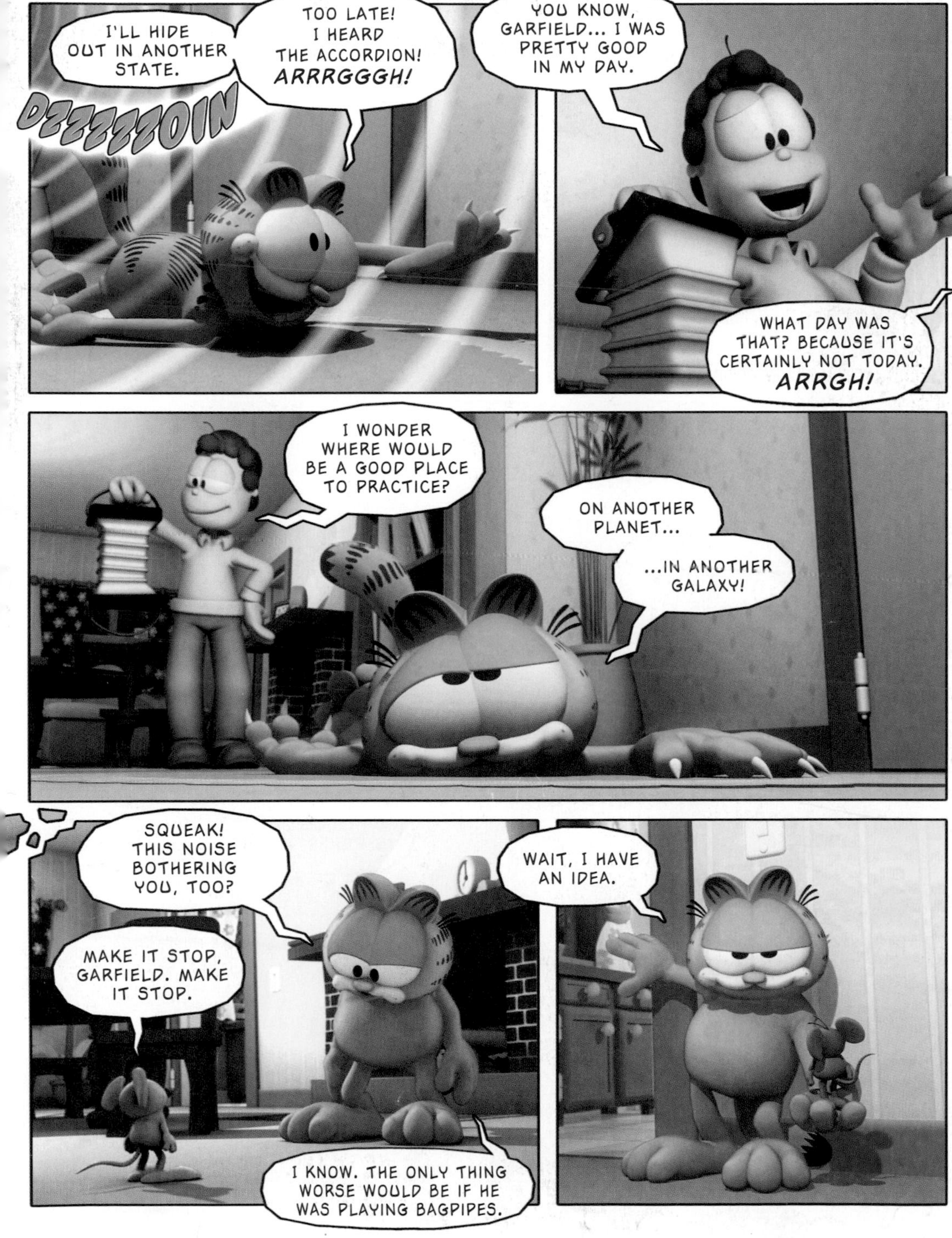
I'LL HIDE OUT IN ANOTHER STATE.
DZZZZZOIN
TOO LATE! I HEARD THE ACCORDION! ARRRGGGH!
YOU KNOW, GARFIELD... I WAS PRETTY GOOD IN MY DAY.
WHAT DAY WAS THAT? BECAUSE IT'S CERTAINLY NOT TODAY. ARRGH!
I WONDER WHERE WOULD BE A GOOD PLACE TO PRACTICE?
ON ANOTHER PLANET...
...IN ANOTHER GALAXY!
SQUEAK! THIS NOISE BOTHERING YOU, TOO?
MAKE IT STOP, GARFIELD. MAKE IT STOP.
I KNOW. THE ONLY THING WORSE WOULD BE IF HE WAS PLAYING BAGPIPES.
WAIT, I HAVE AN IDEA.

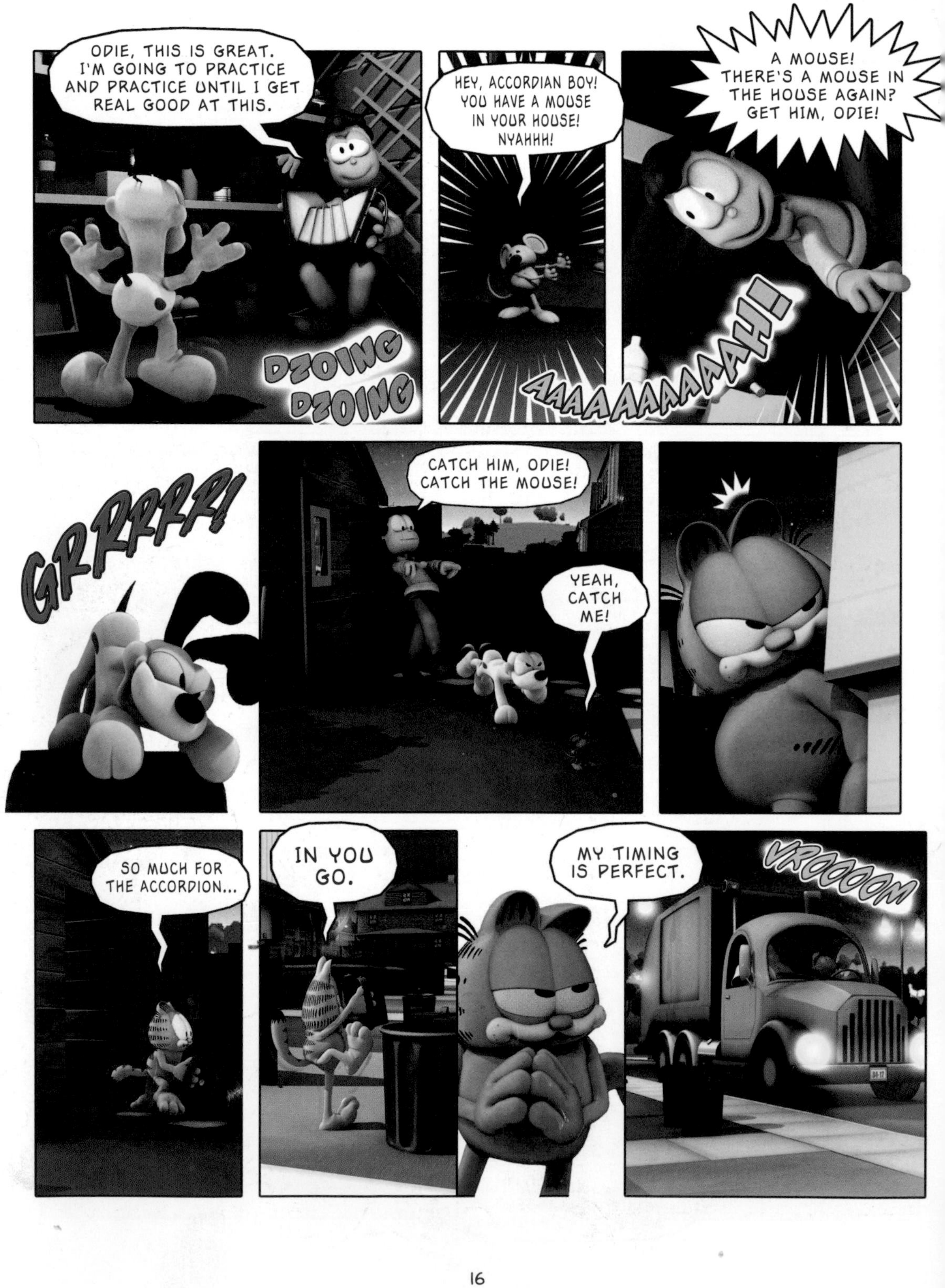

ODIE, THIS IS GREAT. I'M GOING TO PRACTICE AND PRACTICE UNTIL I GET REAL GOOD AT THIS.
DZOING DZOING
HEY, ACCORDIAN BOY! YOU HAVE A MOUSE IN YOUR HOUSE! NYAHHH!
A MOUSE! THERE'S A MOUSE IN THE HOUSE AGAIN? GET HIM, ODIE!
AAAAAAAAAAH!!
GRRRRR!
CATCH HIM, ODIE! CATCH THE MOUSE!
YEAH, CATCH ME!
SO MUCH FOR THE ACCORDION...
IN YOU GO.
MY TIMING IS PERFECT.
VROOOOM

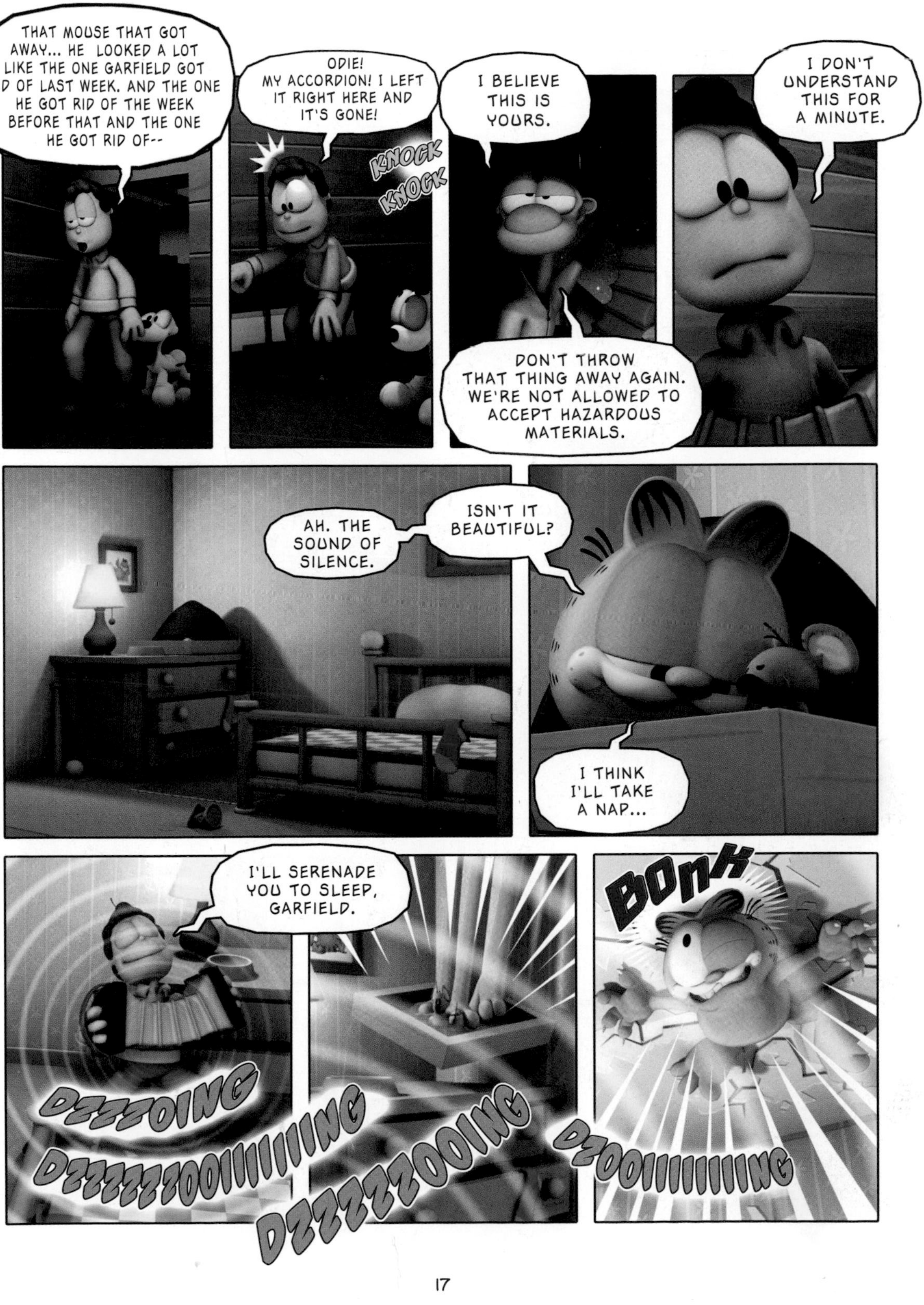
THAT MOUSE THAT GOT AWAY... HE LOOKED A LOT LIKE THE ONE GARFIELD GOT RID OF LAST WEEK. AND THE ONE HE GOT RID OF THE WEEK BEFORE THAT AND THE ONE HE GOT RID OF--
ODIE! MY ACCORDION! I LEFT IT RIGHT HERE AND IT'S GONE!
KNOCK KNOCK
I BELIEVE THIS IS YOURS.
DON'T THROW THAT THING AWAY AGAIN. WE'RE NOT ALLOWED TO ACCEPT HAZARDOUS MATERIALS.
I DON'T UNDERSTAND THIS FOR A MINUTE.
AH. THE SOUND OF SILENCE.
ISN'T IT BEAUTIFUL?
I THINK I'LL TAKE A NAP...
I'LL SERENADE YOU TO SLEEP, GARFIELD.
DZZZOING
DZZZZZZOOIIIIIIIING
DZZZZZZOOING
DZOOIIIIIIIIING
BONK

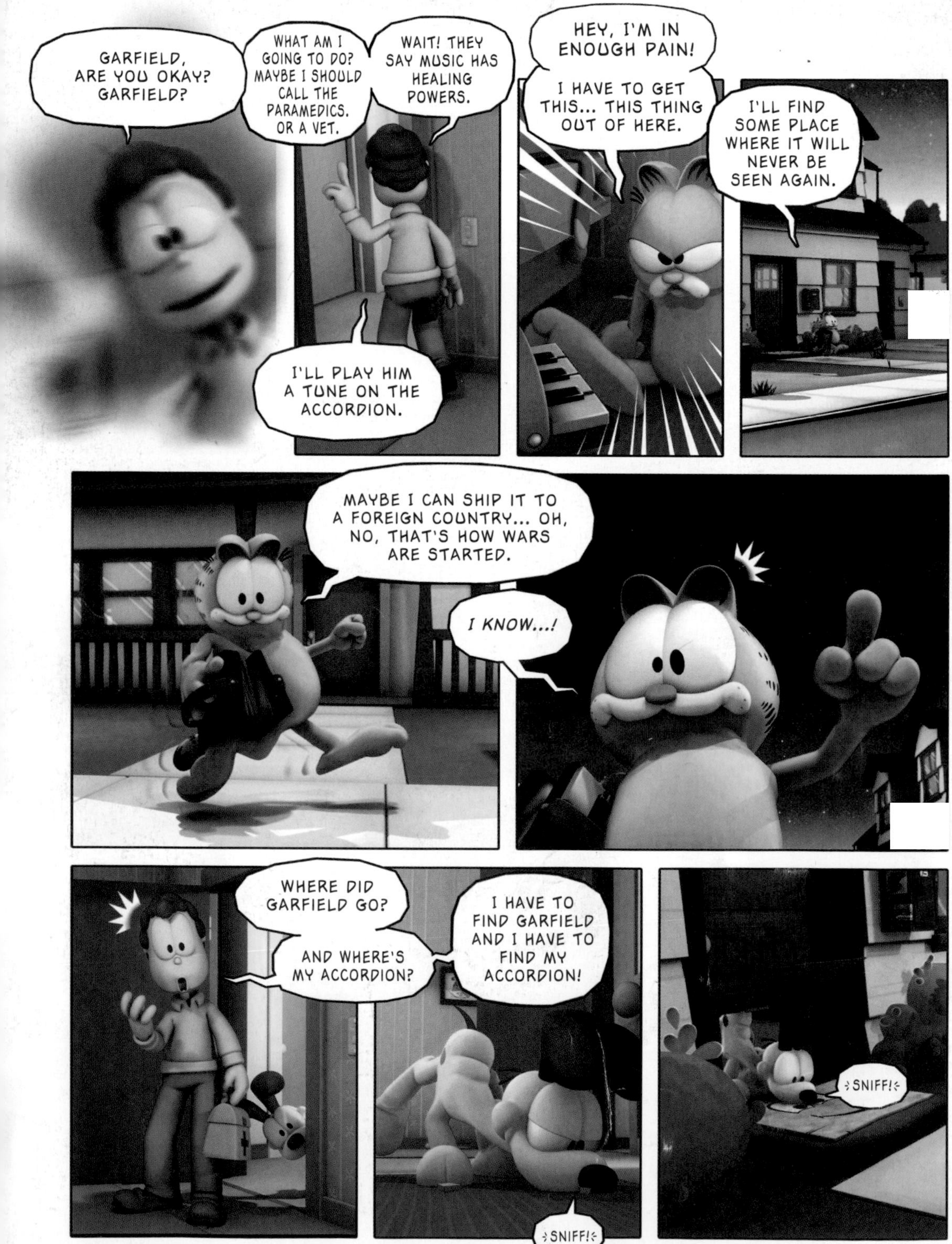
GARFIELD, ARE YOU OKAY? GARFIELD?
WHAT AM I GOING TO DO? MAYBE I SHOULD CALL THE PARAMEDICS. OR A VET.
WAIT! THEY SAY MUSIC HAS HEALING POWERS.
I'LL PLAY HIM A TUNE ON THE ACCORDION.
HEY, I'M IN ENOUGH PAIN!
I HAVE TO GET THIS... THIS THING OUT OF HERE.
I'LL FIND SOME PLACE WHERE IT WILL NEVER BE SEEN AGAIN.
MAYBE I CAN SHIP IT TO A FOREIGN COUNTRY... OH, NO, THAT'S HOW WARS ARE STARTED.
I KNOW...!
WHERE DID GARFIELD GO?
AND WHERE'S MY ACCORDION?
I HAVE TO FIND GARFIELD AND I HAVE TO FIND MY ACCORDION!
SNIFF!
SNIFF!

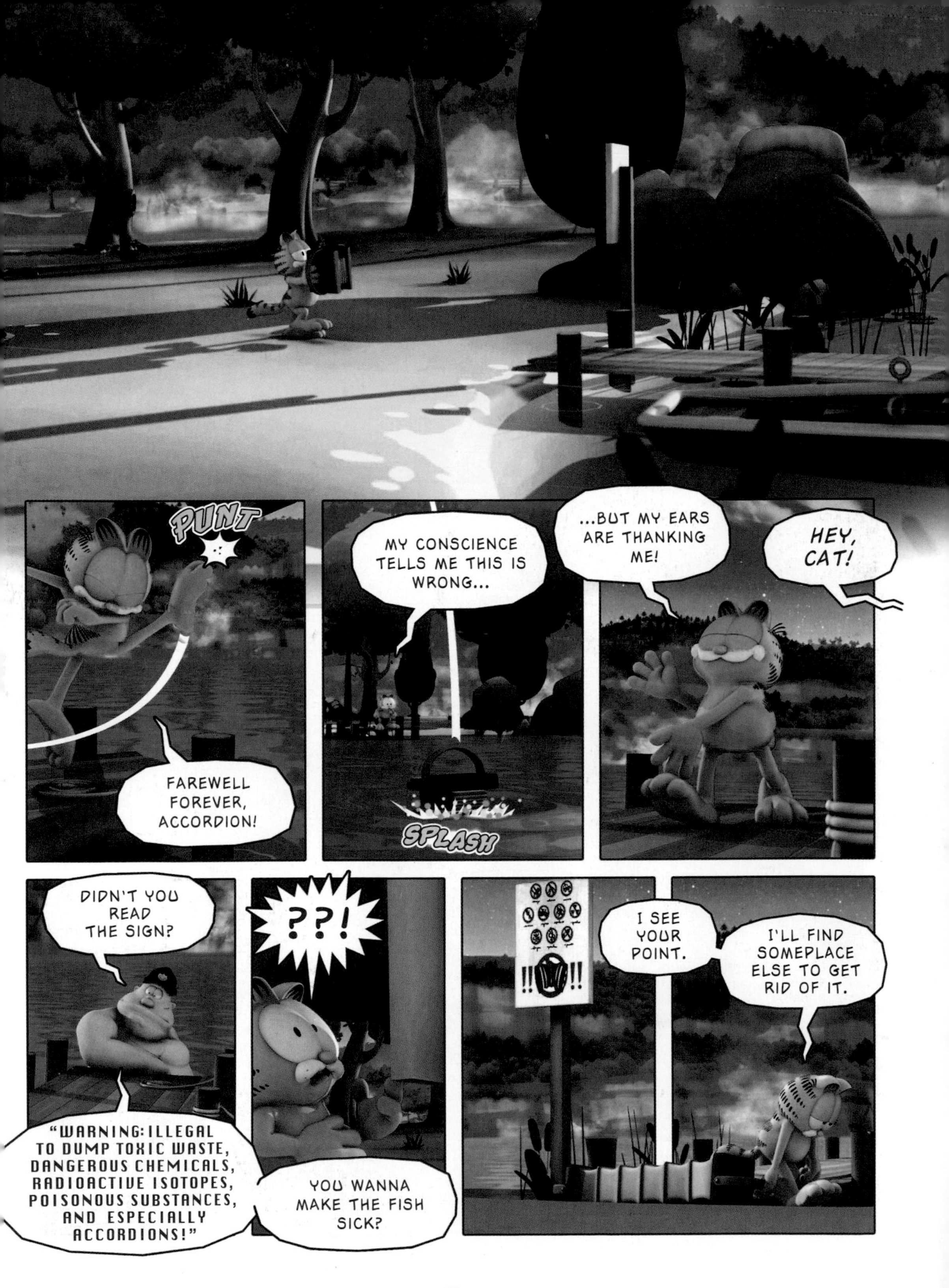
PUNT
FAREWELL FOREVER, ACCORDION!
MY CONSCIENCE TELLS ME THIS IS WRONG...
SPLASH
...BUT MY EARS ARE THANKING ME!
HEY, CAT!
DIDN'T YOU READ THE SIGN?
"WARNING: ILLEGAL TO DUMP TOXIC WASTE, DANGEROUS CHEMICALS, RADIOACTIVE ISOTOPES, POISONOUS SUBSTANCES, AND ESPECIALLY ACCORDIONS!"
??!
YOU WANNA MAKE THE FISH SICK?
I SEE YOUR POINT.
I'LL FIND SOMEPLACE ELSE TO GET RID OF IT.

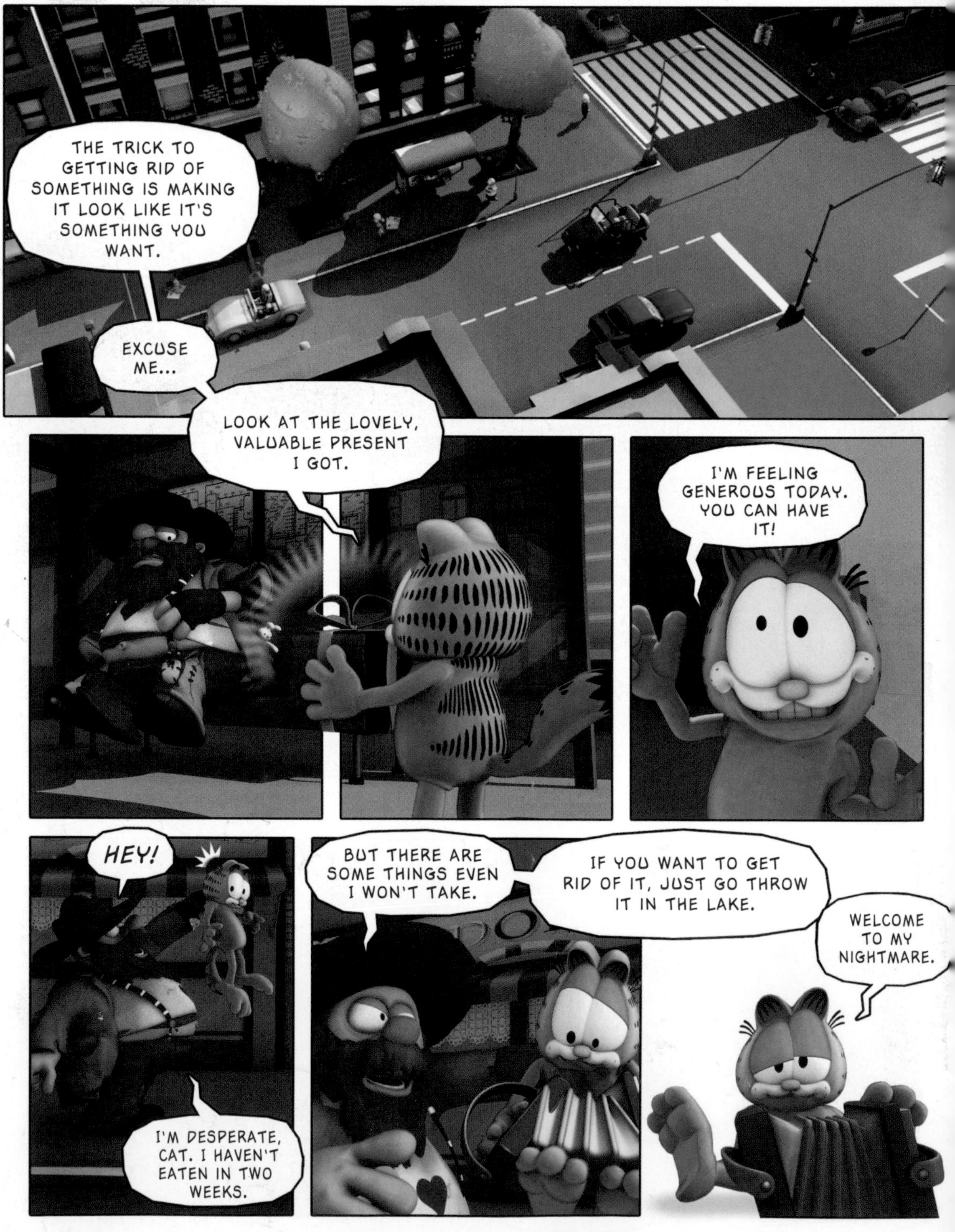
THE TRICK TO GETTING RID OF SOMETHING IS MAKING IT LOOK LIKE IT'S SOMETHING YOU WANT.
EXCUSE ME...
LOOK AT THE LOVELY, VALUABLE PRESENT I GOT.
I'M FEELING GENEROUS TODAY. YOU CAN HAVE IT!
HEY!
I'M DESPERATE, CAT. I HAVEN'T EATEN IN TWO WEEKS.
BUT THERE ARE SOME THINGS EVEN I WON'T TAKE.
IF YOU WANT TO GET RID OF IT, JUST GO THROW IT IN THE LAKE.
WELCOME TO MY NIGHTMARE.

A CONSTRUCTION SITE!

THIS IS MY LAST CHANCE!

IN YOU GO!

BLANG BLANG BLANG BLANG

BLANG BLANG BLANG BLANG

IT'S DONE!

NOW, I'LL NEVER SEE THAT INSTRUMENT OF EVIL AGAIN.

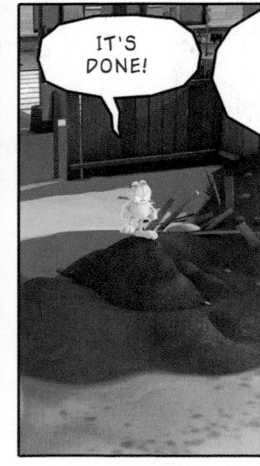

→SNIFF!←
→SNIFF!←

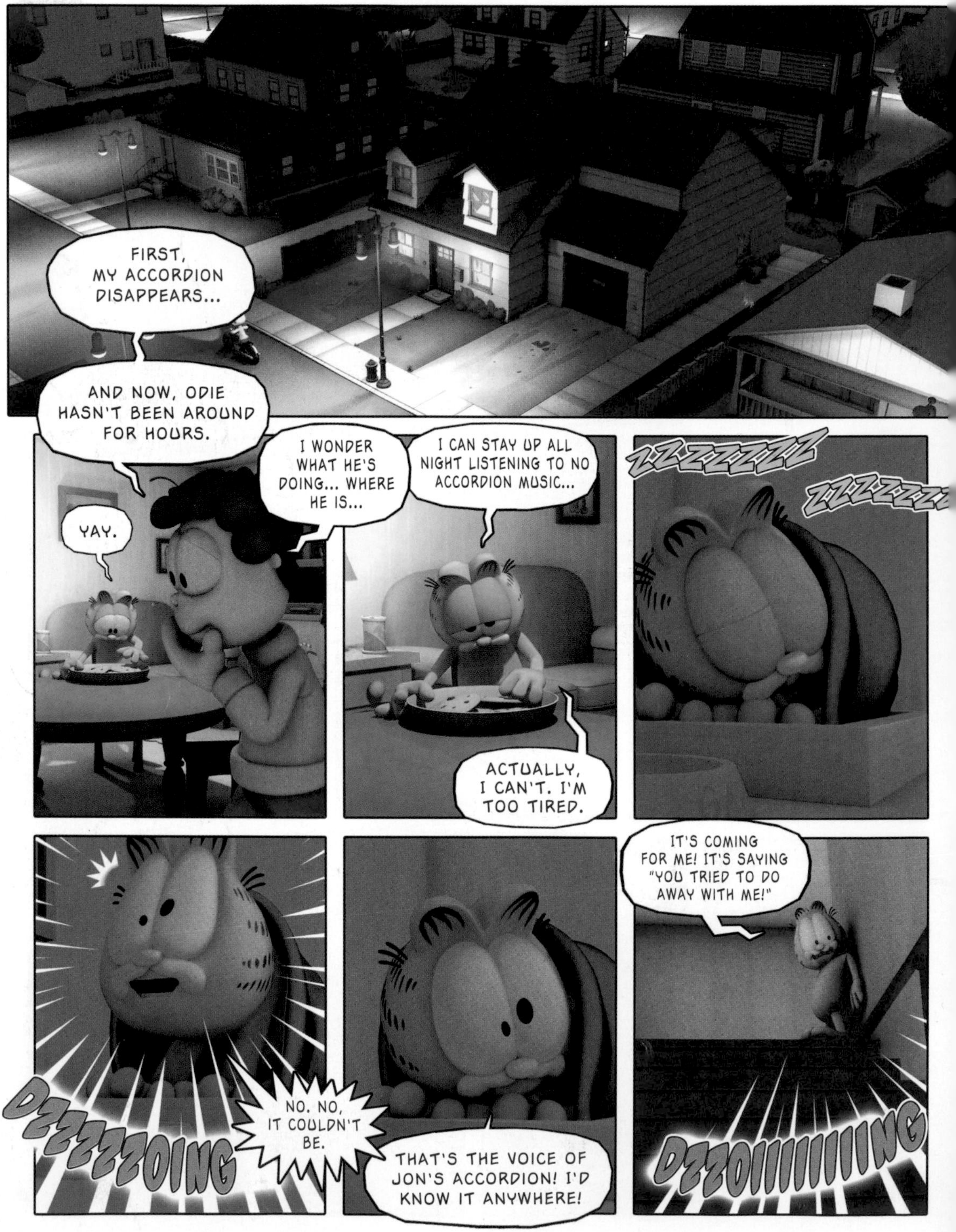
FIRST, MY ACCORDION DISAPPEARS...
AND NOW, ODIE HASN'T BEEN AROUND FOR HOURS.
YAY.
I WONDER WHAT HE'S DOING... WHERE HE IS...
I CAN STAY UP ALL NIGHT LISTENING TO NO ACCORDION MUSIC...
ACTUALLY, I CAN'T. I'M TOO TIRED.
ZZZZZZZZ
NO. NO, IT COULDN'T BE.
DZZZZZOING
THAT'S THE VOICE OF JON'S ACCORDION! I'D KNOW IT ANYWHERE!
IT'S COMING FOR ME! IT'S SAYING "YOU TRIED TO DO AWAY WITH ME!"
DZZOIIIIIIIING

DZZOIIIIIIIIING

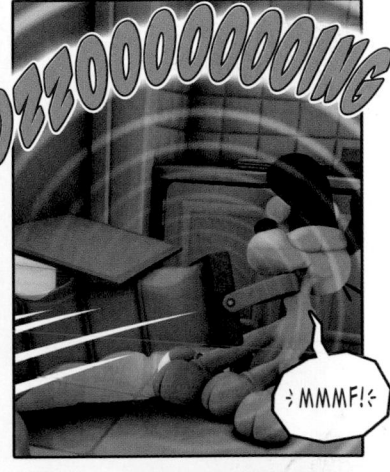

DZZOOOOOOOOING

«MMMF!»

THERE'S NOTHING THERE. IT'S JUST MY IMAGINATION.

I'LL SEE FOR MYSELF AND THEN I'LL BE ABLE TO GO BACK TO SLEEP...

DZZZZOING

?

DZOOOING

NO, NO! I BURIED YOU! I KNOW I DID!

WHAT'S GOING ON IN HERE?

ODIE! IT'S YOU... AND MY ACCORDION!

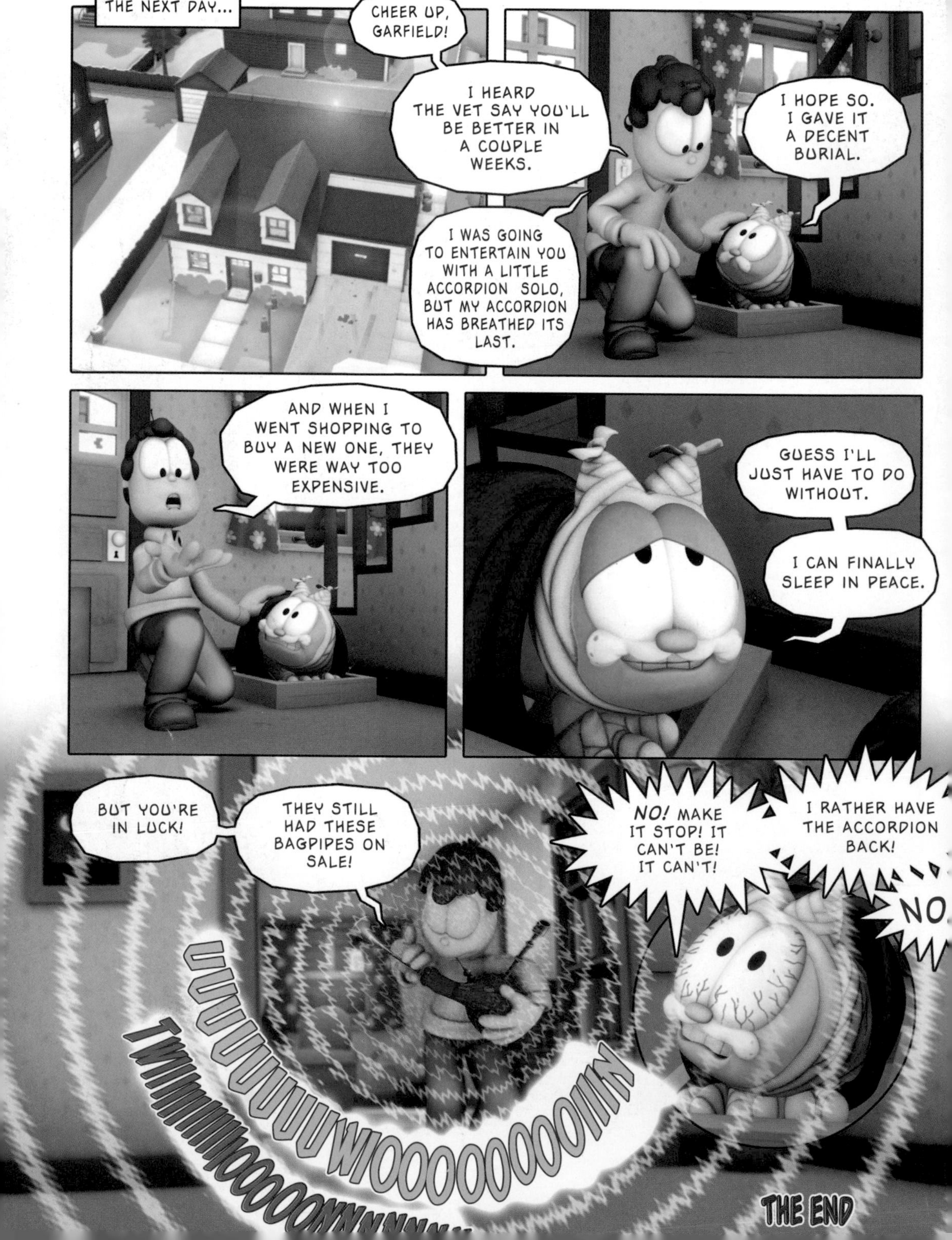
THE NEXT DAY...
CHEER UP, GARFIELD!
I HEARD THE VET SAY YOU'LL BE BETTER IN A COUPLE WEEKS.
I WAS GOING TO ENTERTAIN YOU WITH A LITTLE ACCORDION SOLO, BUT MY ACCORDION HAS BREATHED ITS LAST.
I HOPE SO. I GAVE IT A DECENT BURIAL.
AND WHEN I WENT SHOPPING TO BUY A NEW ONE, THEY WERE WAY TOO EXPENSIVE.
GUESS I'LL JUST HAVE TO DO WITHOUT.
I CAN FINALLY SLEEP IN PEACE.
BUT YOU'RE IN LUCK!
THEY STILL HAD THESE BAGPIPES ON SALE!
TWIIIIIIIIOOOOONNNNNN... UUUUUUUUWIOOOOOOOOIIIN
NO! MAKE IT STOP! IT CAN'T BE! IT CAN'T!
I RATHER HAVE THE ACCORDION BACK!
NO
THE END

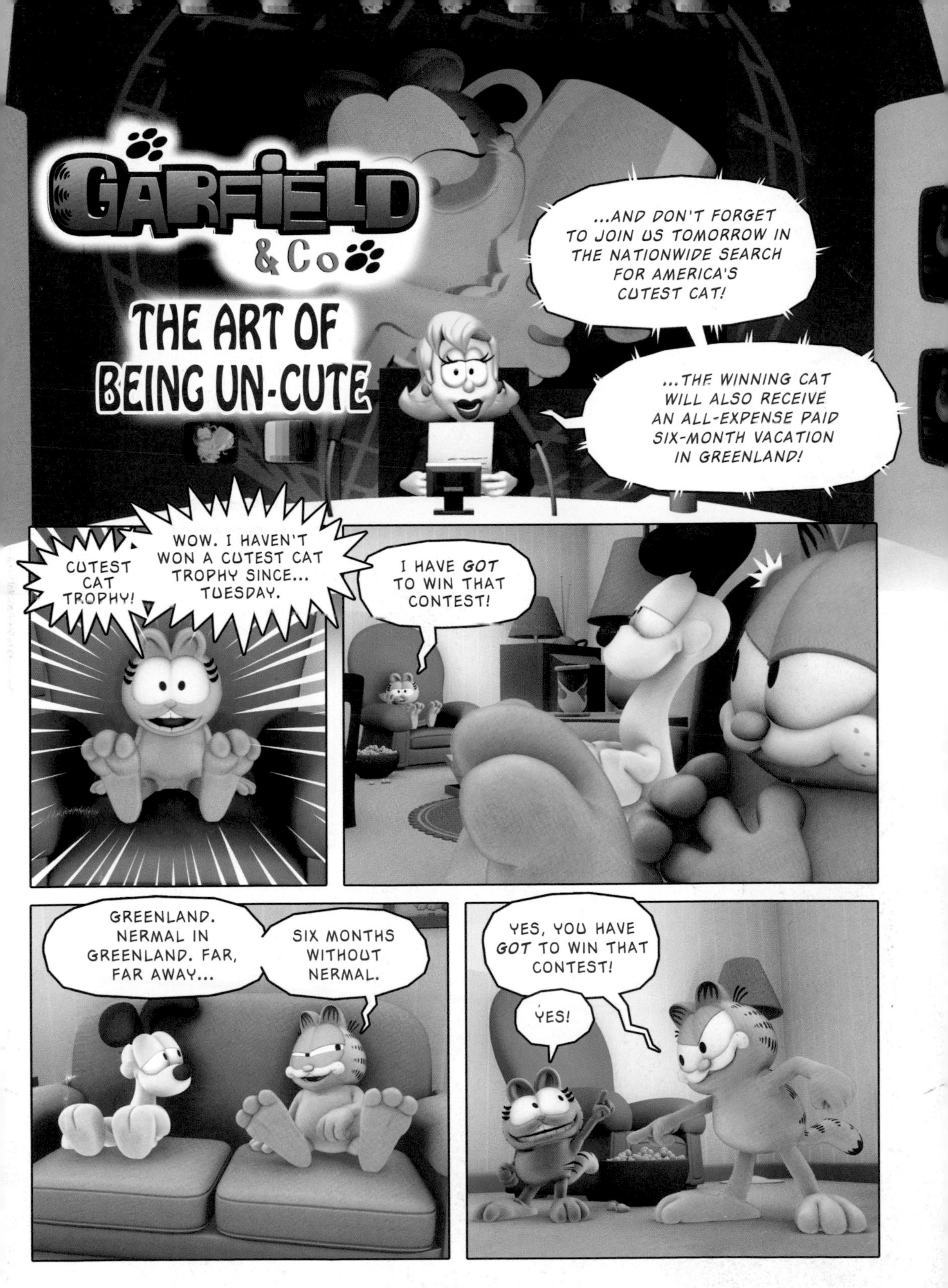
GARFIELD & Co
THE ART OF BEING UN-CUTE
...AND DON'T FORGET TO JOIN US TOMORROW IN THE NATIONWIDE SEARCH FOR AMERICA'S CUTEST CAT!
...THE WINNING CAT WILL ALSO RECEIVE AN ALL-EXPENSE PAID SIX-MONTH VACATION IN GREENLAND!
CUTEST CAT TROPHY!
WOW. I HAVEN'T WON A CUTEST CAT TROPHY SINCE... TUESDAY.
I HAVE *GOT* TO WIN THAT CONTEST!
GREENLAND. NERMAL IN GREENLAND. FAR, FAR AWAY...
SIX MONTHS WITHOUT NERMAL.
YES, YOU HAVE *GOT* TO WIN THAT CONTEST!
YES!

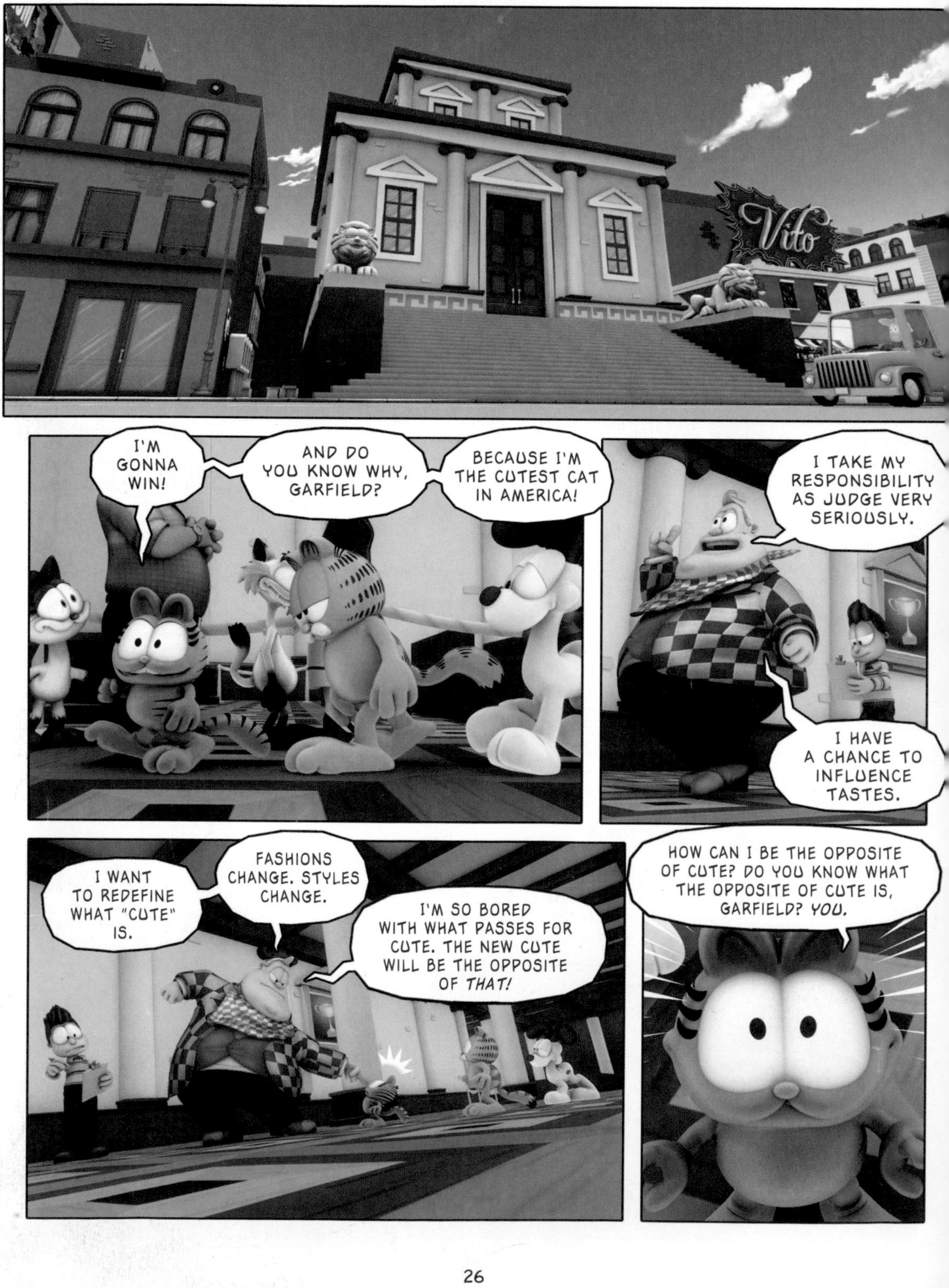
Vito
I'M GONNA WIN!
AND DO YOU KNOW WHY, GARFIELD?
BECAUSE I'M THE CUTEST CAT IN AMERICA!
I TAKE MY RESPONSIBILITY AS JUDGE VERY SERIOUSLY.
I HAVE A CHANCE TO INFLUENCE TASTES.
I WANT TO REDEFINE WHAT "CUTE" IS.
FASHIONS CHANGE. STYLES CHANGE.
I'M SO BORED WITH WHAT PASSES FOR CUTE. THE NEW CUTE WILL BE THE OPPOSITE OF *THAT!*
HOW CAN I BE THE OPPOSITE OF CUTE? DO YOU KNOW WHAT THE OPPOSITE OF CUTE IS, GARFIELD? *YOU.*

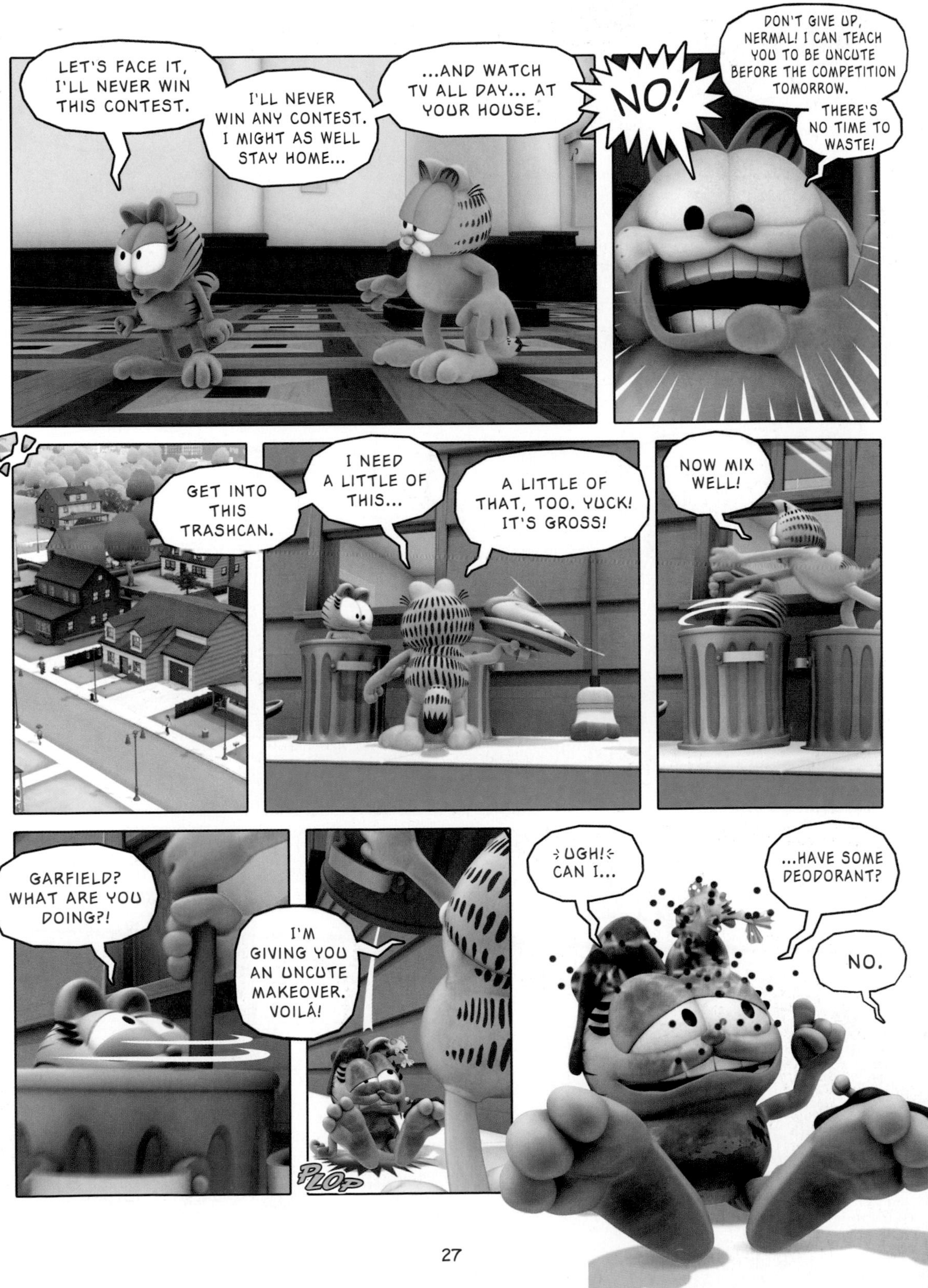
LET'S FACE IT, I'LL NEVER WIN THIS CONTEST.
I'LL NEVER WIN ANY CONTEST. I MIGHT AS WELL STAY HOME...
...AND WATCH TV ALL DAY... AT YOUR HOUSE.
NO!
DON'T GIVE UP, NERMAL! I CAN TEACH YOU TO BE UNCUTE BEFORE THE COMPETITION TOMORROW.
THERE'S NO TIME TO WASTE!
GET INTO THIS TRASHCAN.
I NEED A LITTLE OF THIS...
A LITTLE OF THAT, TOO. YUCK! IT'S GROSS!
NOW MIX WELL!
GARFIELD? WHAT ARE YOU DOING?!
I'M GIVING YOU AN UNCUTE MAKEOVER. VOILÁ!
PLOP
UGH! CAN I...
...HAVE SOME DEODORANT?
NO.

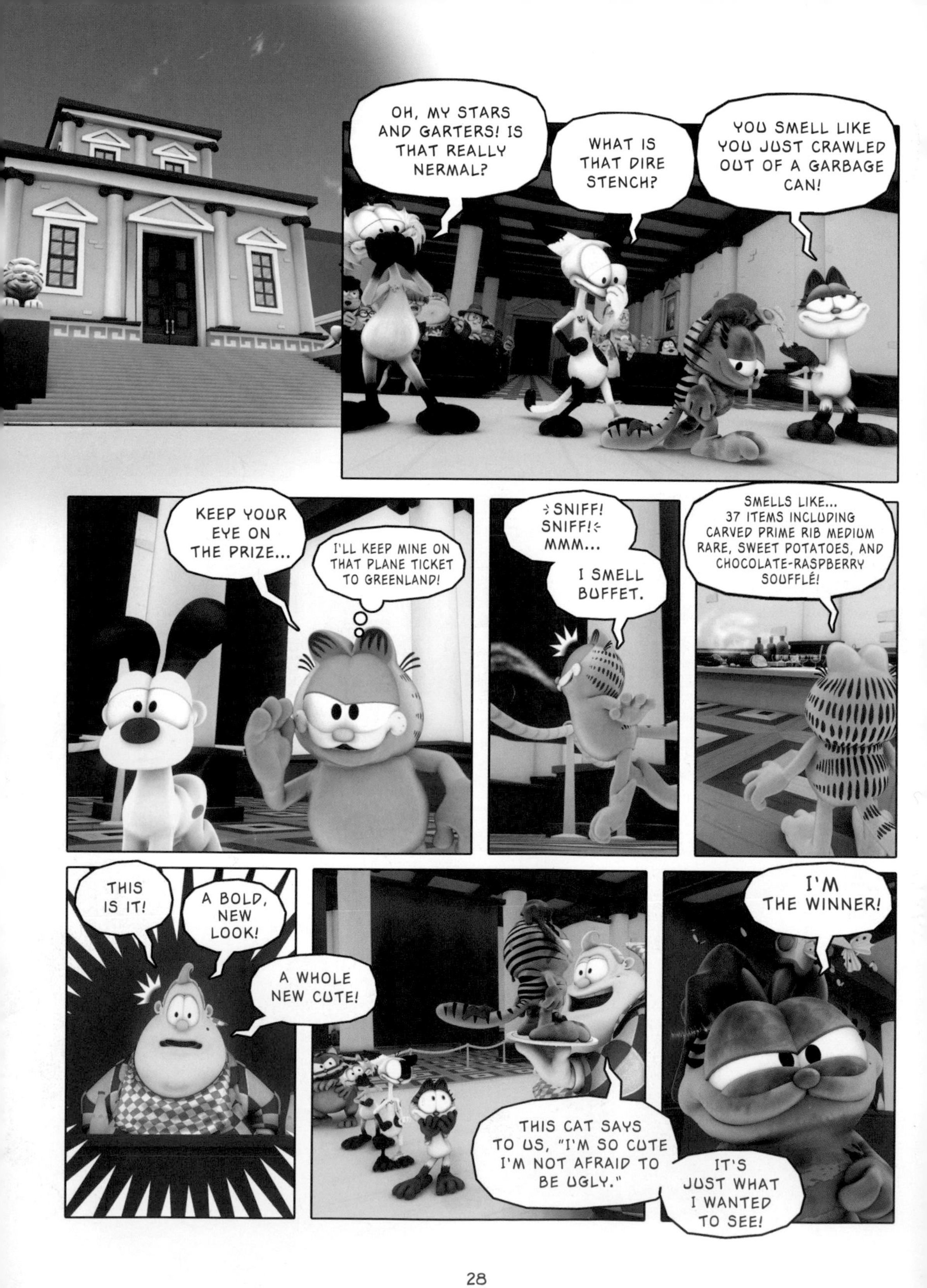
OH, MY STARS AND GARTERS! IS THAT REALLY NERMAL?
WHAT IS THAT DIRE STENCH?
YOU SMELL LIKE YOU JUST CRAWLED OUT OF A GARBAGE CAN!
KEEP YOUR EYE ON THE PRIZE...
I'LL KEEP MINE ON THAT PLANE TICKET TO GREENLAND!
SNIFF! SNIFF! MMM...
I SMELL BUFFET.
SMELLS LIKE... 37 ITEMS INCLUDING CARVED PRIME RIB MEDIUM RARE, SWEET POTATOES, AND CHOCOLATE-RASPBERRY SOUFFLÉ!
THIS IS IT!
A BOLD, NEW LOOK!
A WHOLE NEW CUTE!
THIS CAT SAYS TO US, "I'M SO CUTE I'M NOT AFRAID TO BE UGLY."
IT'S JUST WHAT I WANTED TO SEE!
I'M THE WINNER!

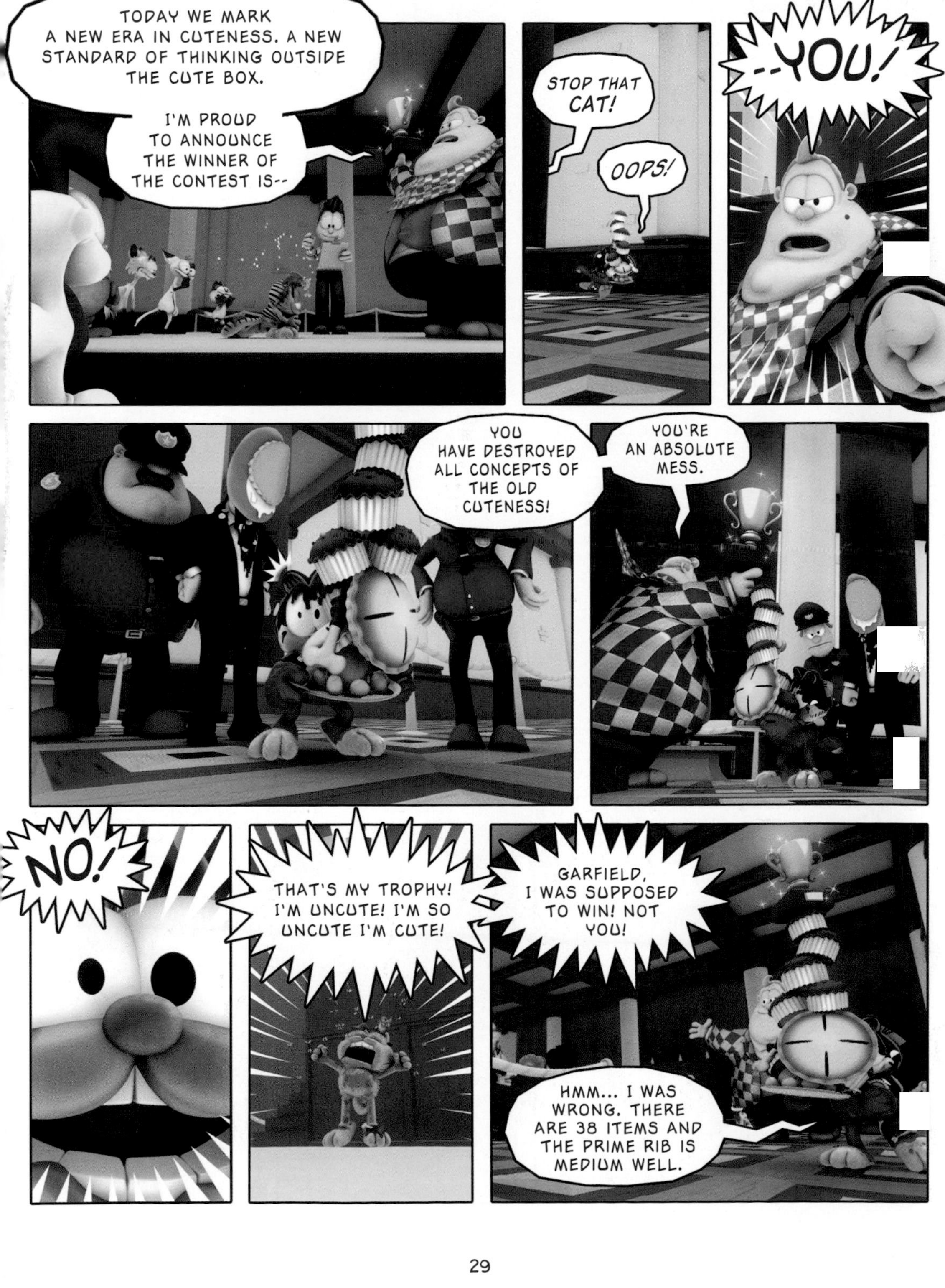
TODAY WE MARK A NEW ERA IN CUTENESS. A NEW STANDARD OF THINKING OUTSIDE THE CUTE BOX.
I'M PROUD TO ANNOUNCE THE WINNER OF THE CONTEST IS--
STOP THAT CAT!
OOPS!
--YOU!
YOU HAVE DESTROYED ALL CONCEPTS OF THE OLD CUTENESS!
YOU'RE AN ABSOLUTE MESS.
NO!
THAT'S MY TROPHY! I'M UNCUTE! I'M SO UNCUTE I'M CUTE!
GARFIELD, I WAS SUPPOSED TO WIN! NOT YOU!
HMM... I WAS WRONG. THERE ARE 38 ITEMS AND THE PRIME RIB IS MEDIUM WELL.

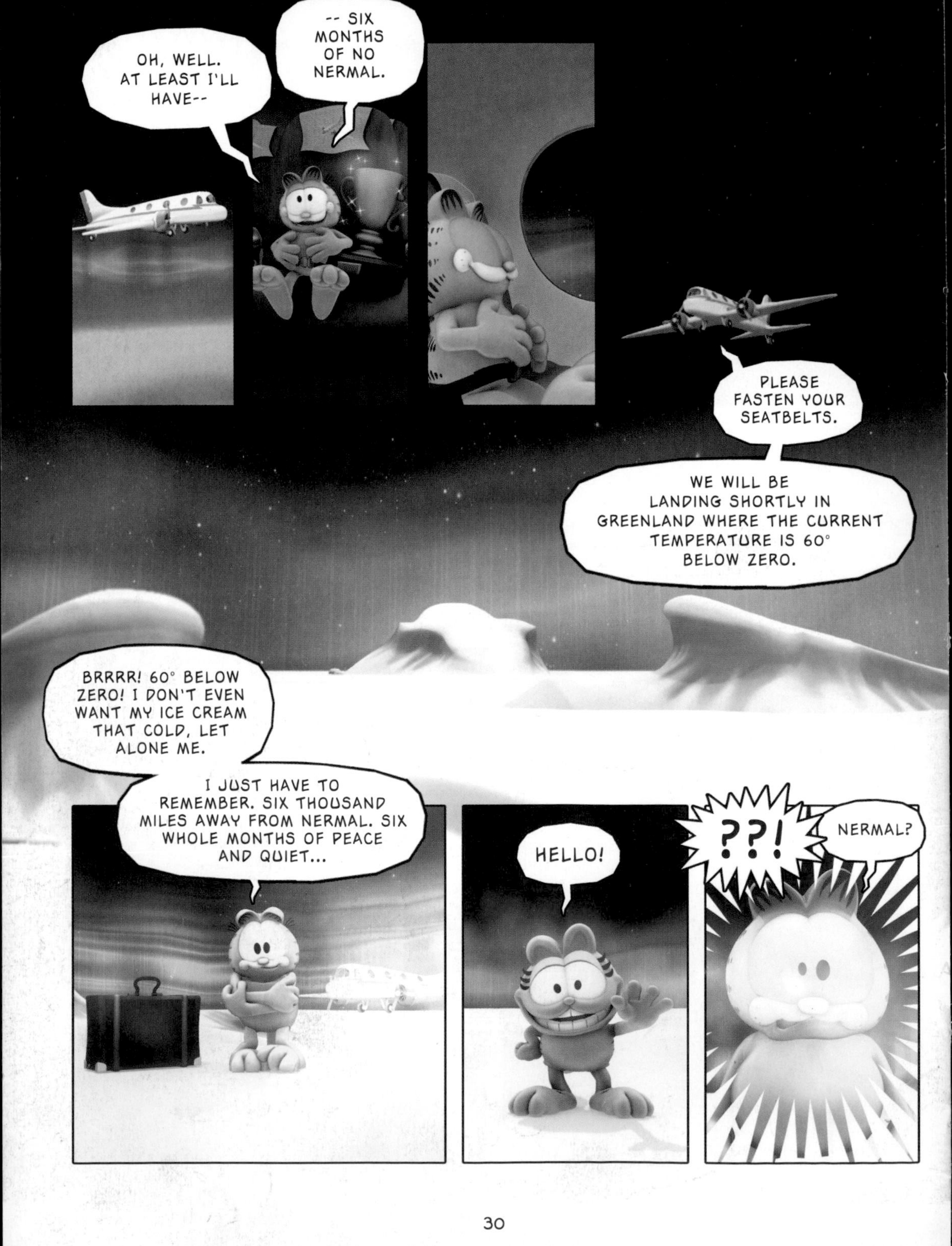
OH, WELL. AT LEAST I'LL HAVE--
-- SIX MONTHS OF NO NERMAL.
PLEASE FASTEN YOUR SEATBELTS.
WE WILL BE LANDING SHORTLY IN GREENLAND WHERE THE CURRENT TEMPERATURE IS 60° BELOW ZERO.
BRRRR! 60° BELOW ZERO! I DON'T EVEN WANT MY ICE CREAM THAT COLD, LET ALONE ME.
I JUST HAVE TO REMEMBER. SIX THOUSAND MILES AWAY FROM NERMAL. SIX WHOLE MONTHS OF PEACE AND QUIET...
HELLO!
??!
NERMAL?

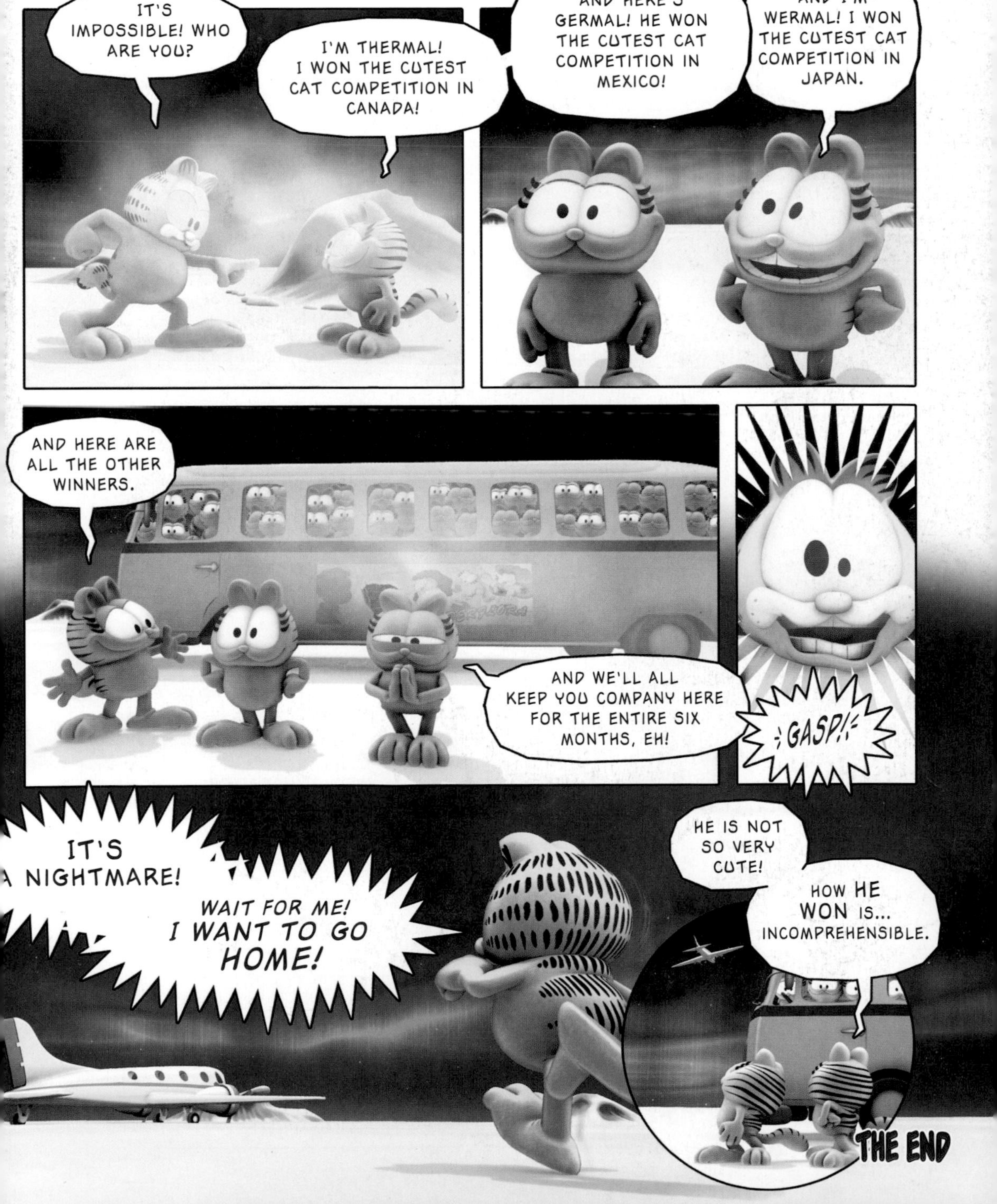
IT'S IMPOSSIBLE! WHO ARE YOU?
I'M THERMAL! I WON THE CUTEST CAT COMPETITION IN CANADA!
AND HERE'S GERMAL! HE WON THE CUTEST CAT COMPETITION IN MEXICO!
AND I'M WERMAL! I WON THE CUTEST CAT COMPETITION IN JAPAN.
AND HERE ARE ALL THE OTHER WINNERS.
AND WE'LL ALL KEEP YOU COMPANY HERE FOR THE ENTIRE SIX MONTHS, EH!
GASP!
IT'S A NIGHTMARE!
WAIT FOR ME! I WANT TO GO HOME!
HE IS NOT SO VERY CUTE!
HOW HE WON IS... INCOMPREHENSIBLE.
THE END

WATCH OUT FOR PAPERCUTZ™

WELCOME TO THE EPIC, ESPIONAGE-LADEN EIGHTH GARFIELD & CO GRAPHIC NOVEL FROM PAPERCUTZ. WE'RE THE FOLKS DEDICATED TO PUBLISHING GREAT GRAPHIC NOVELS FOR ALL AGES. I'M YOUR MUSIC-LOVING EDITOR-IN-CHIEF, JIM SALICRUP.

BEFORE I GET TO OUR BIG ANNOUNCEMENT, I MUST SAY A WORD OR TWO IN DEFENSE OF ACCORDIONS AND BAGPIPES. WHILE THE LASAGNA-LOVING STAR OF THIS SERIES OF GRAPHIC NOVELS IS CERTAINLY ENTITLED TO HIS OPINION, NO MATTER HOW CLOSED-MINDED IT MAY BE, IT DOESN'T NECESSARILY REFLECT THE VIEWS OF THE FAR MORE OPEN-MINDED EDITORIAL STAFF AT PAPERCUTZ. REGARDING THE OFT-MALIGNED ACCORDION, ONE OF MY FAVORITE CABARET PERFORMERS IS THE AWESOMELY-TALENTED, DOWN-RIGHT PHENOMENAL PHOEBE LEGERE. WHILE KNOWN FOR HER EXCELLENT PORTRAYAL OF THE BEAUTIFUL CLAIRE, THE BLIND ACCORDION-PLAYING SWEETHEART OF TOXIE, IN THE CLASSIC TROMA FILMS, THE TOXIC AVENGER PART II AND THE TOXIC AVENGER PART III THE LAST TEMPTATION OF TOXIE (NOT TO BE CONFUSED WITH A THE SIMILAR CHARACTER IN THE TOXIC CRUSADERS ANIMATED SERIES, WHO WAS A VERY POOR ACCORDION PLAYER), PHOEBE IS AN ACCOMPLISHED MUSICIAN, WHO HAS PROVEN TIME AND TIME AGAIN HOW SUBLIME AND ELEGANT AN INSTRUMENT THE ACCORDION CAN BE... WHEN IN THE RIGHT HANDS.

AS FOR BAGPIPES... HOW CAN GARFIELD NOT LOVE BAGPIPES? AS SCOTTY PROVED PLAYING AMAZING GRACE AT SPOCK'S BURIAL IN SPACE IN STAR TREK: THE WRATH OF KAHN, THE BAGPIPES ARE AN INSTRUMENT THAT CAN EASILY EVOKE DEEP EMOTIONS. PAUL McCARTNEY CERTAINLY KNEW THAT WHEN HE COMPOSED MULL OF THE FANGPYRE*, ER, I MEAN MULL OF KINTYRE.

BUT IT REALLY DOESN'T MATTER WHETHER GARFIELD AND I AGREE. WE CAN STILL LOVE EACH OTHER DESPITE OUR DIFFERENCES. AS THE AFOREMENTIONED EX-BEATLE ONCE SANG "WE CAN WORK IT OUT."

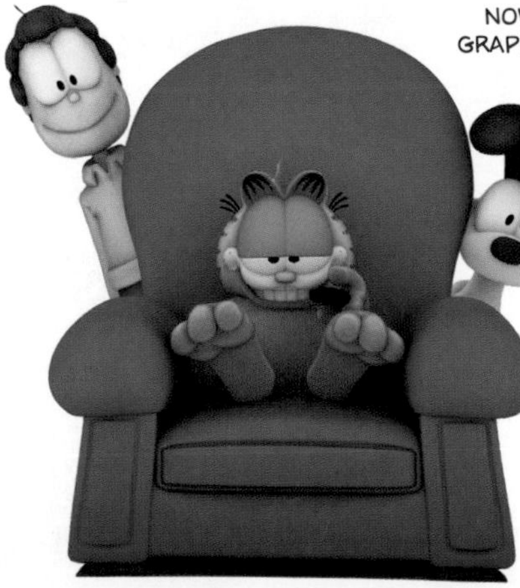

NOW FOR OUR BIG ANNOUNCEMENT! GARFIELD & CO #8 IS THE LAST GRAPHIC NOVEL IN THIS SERIES. BUT WE'RE MORE THAN HAPPY TO ANNOUNCE THAT A SERIES OF THE GARFIELD SHOW GRAPHIC NOVELS IS SOON FORTHCOMING FROM PAPERCUTZ! MERE MONTHS FROM NOW YOU'LL BE ABLE TO PURCHASE GARFIELD GRAPHIC NOVELS IN BOTH HARDCOVER EDITIONS AND, FOR THE FIRST TIME, PAPERBACKS AS WELL! AND HERE'S THE BEST PART—THE GARFIELD SHOW GRAPHIC NOVELS WILL CONTAIN TWICE AS MANY PAGES OF GARFIELD COMICS!

SOME OF THE MORE CYNICAL AMONGST YOU MIGHT BE THINKING, "I BET THAT'S JUST AN EXCUSE TO JACK THE PRICE UP!" GUESS WHAT? YOU'LL BE ABLE TO GET THE GARFIELD SHOW GRAPHIC NOVEL PAPERBACK, WITH TWICE AS MANY PAGES, AT THE EXACT SAME PRICE AS THIS GRAPHIC NOVEL! IS THAT A GREAT DEAL OR WHAT? ESPECIALLY IN THESE DIFFICULT TIMES!

UNTIL NEXT TIME, DON'T FORGET THAT IT'S NEVER TOO LATE TO TAKE UP A MUSICAL INSTRUMENT, SAY, AN ACCORDION OR THE BAGPIPES...?

JIM

*OOPS! I MUST'VE CONFUSED THAT CLASSIC WINGS TUNE WITH THE TITLE OF ONE OF THE BEST-SELLING PAPERCUTZ GRAPHIC NOVELS EVER—LEGO® NINJAGO #4 "TOMB OF THE FANGPYRE."

STAY IN TOUCH!

EMAIL: salicrup@papercutz.com
WEB: www.papercutz.com
TWITTER: @papercutzgn
FACEBOOK: PAPERCUTZGRAPHICNOVELS
SNAIL MAIL: Papercutz, 160 Broadway, Suite 700, East Wing, New York, NY 10038